AN ACCOMMODATING HUSBAND

FENELLA J. MILLER

Boldwood

First published in 2017. This edition published in Great Britain in 2025 by Boldwood Books Ltd.

Copyright © Fenella J. Miller, 2017

Cover Design by Colin Thomas

Cover Images: Colin Thomas and Alamy

The moral right of Fenella J. Miller to be identified as the author of this work has been asserted in accordance with the Copyright, Designs and Patents Act 1988.

All rights reserved. No part of this book may be reproduced in any form or by any electronic or mechanical means, including information storage and retrieval systems, without written permission from the author, except for the use of brief quotations in a book review. This book is a work of fiction and, except in the case of historical fact, any resemblance to actual persons, living or dead, is purely coincidental.

Every effort has been made to obtain the necessary permissions with reference to copyright material, both illustrative and quoted. We apologise for any omissions in this respect and will be pleased to make the appropriate acknowledgements in any future edition.

A CIP catalogue record for this book is available from the British Library.

Paperback ISBN 978-1-83678-325-1

Large Print ISBN 978-1-83678-324-4

Hardback ISBN 978-1-83678-323-7

Ebook ISBN 978-1-83678-326-8

Kindle ISBN 978-1-83678-327-5

Audio CD ISBN 978-1-83678-318-3

MP3 CD ISBN 978-1-83678-319-0

Digital audio download ISBN 978-1-83678-322-0

This book is printed on certified sustainable paper. Boldwood Books is dedicated to putting sustainability at the heart of our business. For more information please visit https://www.boldwoodbooks.com/about-us/sustainability/

Boldwood Books Ltd, 23 Bowerdean Street, London, SW6 3TN

www.boldwoodbooks.com

1

CASTLEMERE, ESSEX, APRIL 1814

'His grace, the Duke of Silchester, my lord.' The butler – Beau misremembered his name – bowed and backed out as if in the presence of royalty.

'What brings you here, my friend? It's not often you venture down to visit me at Castlemere.' Rushton's smile was genuine, but the man looked tired and unhappy. He had not stood up to greet him.

'I was concerned about you, old fellow. I've not seen you since – well – it's so long ago I can scarcely recall the date.' Beau strode across and took a seat opposite without being asked. 'You were invited to spend Christmas at Silchester with your girls, but refused the invitation.'

'I wouldn't inflict those two on anyone. They have run wild these past two years and I've just lost the third governess in as many months. I think I'm going to have to send them away to school and I promised Charlotte on her deathbed that I would never do that.'

'Good God! Are you telling me that you look as miserable as sin because your daughters have got out of hand? Take action,

Rushton, bring them into line even if it means putting them over your knee a few times.'

'That's another thing I gave my word I'd never do. This disaster is entirely my own fault. I should have spent more time here with them and not behaved as if I was a single gentleman like yourself.'

The conversation was interrupted as a footman came in with a laden tray. 'Put it down, and then leave us.' Rushton didn't need to give orders; his staff knew him so well they anticipated his every whim. No doubt a chamber was being prepared for Beau at this very moment.

Beau strolled across and poured them both a cup of coffee. He ignored the pastries. 'Here, drink this and we shall come up with a solution to this problem.'

After three cups, he certainly felt more awake after his long journey, and his friend looked a little better too.

'It's a great shame that my brother Aubrey and his new wife are abroad. Mary has experience with difficult children and would have been ideal to step in and put things right for you.'

'I don't suppose any other member of your family might wish to take them off my hands?' This was said with a wry smile.

'As you know, both my sister and brother are now parents themselves and would not have the time or inclination to step in. However, I have a suggestion that might work for you.'

Rushton wandered over and piled a plate with pastries and tucked into them as if he hadn't eaten for a week. Through a mouthful, he said. 'Go on, I'm waiting to hear your idea.'

'My younger sister, Giselle, and my cousin, Beth, decided not to have another Season in London, which surprised me somewhat.'

'I suppose I'm obliged to ask why...'

'Giselle is not overfond of the crush and noise of Town, but

Beth, two years her junior, is a typical debutante and there's nothing she likes better than a ball or a soirée.' He paused and leaned across to filch one of his friend's pastries. 'I was fully expecting to open the house in Grosvenor Square and be obliged to do the pretty from now until May. However, the girls have decided they wish to go to Bath instead. They say it will be quieter and they have a desire to bathe in the restorative waters of the Pump Room.'

'That's all very well, Silchester, but two things occur to me. One, the Season in Bath does not start until May, and two, I cannot see that the perambulations of your relatives can be of any help to me.'

'Rushton, you are a man of no imagination. What could be better than giving Giselle and Beth the responsibility of your girls? Looking after them will mean they have less time to get into mischief themselves and thus have solved my dilemma as well as yours.'

For a moment his friend didn't answer, then he laughed. 'This is your way of avoiding having to spend several months in Bath, isn't it? I fear your girls will be disappointed – the town is elegant but no longer as fashionable as it was in the days of Nash. I believe they will find it mostly populated by older ladies and gentlemen nowadays.'

'Which is why I gave my permission immediately for them to go. I have already set things in motion and my man of business has managed to rent a substantial house in the most prestigious district. It comes fully staffed and is, I am assured, no more than a stone's throw from the Pump Room.'

'Are you suggesting that neither of us go with them? Isn't that rather rash?'

'I think we should let them leave alone but join them after a week or so. I intend to send Carstairs, my man of business, with them and he will keep an eye on things and let us know if there are any difficulties.'

'It is all very well saying your sister and your cousin will take charge of my daughters, but would it not be better to ask them first?'

'Giselle will be delighted and Beth will do as she's told. Much as I love them both, it will be a pleasure to have my home to myself for a while. When Aubrey decided he was to marry Mary I thought I would be lonely on my own in such a large establishment. I fear that after spending a year with a house full of hopeful suitors, a constant stream of supper and dinner parties, plus a house party and the ball we had during the Christmas festivities, I am longing for some peace.'

'I believe you to be a confirmed bachelor, Silchester, and you will be happier without the constant chatter of a female companion. By the way, do you still keep a ladybird in Town?'

'Not that it's any of your damned business, but yes, I do. I'm surprised that you haven't remarried yourself. What your girls need is a sensible woman to take charge of their upbringing.'

'As you know, I was married young to the girl I'd been in love with since a stripling. I could not marry without feeling the same way I did for Charlotte. As that will never happen, I prefer to remain a widower.'

'Do you have a male heir if you do not produce one yourself?'

'I have a cousin who has three sons so there's no danger of the title becoming defunct. To return to the matter in hand – do you intend your sister to meet my daughters before they are foisted upon her?'

Beau shook his head. 'It might be wiser for them not to meet so there is no opportunity for Giselle to change her mind. However, I should like to meet the girls myself whilst

I'm here. Who is taking care of them if the governess has run away?'

'They are in the charge of the remaining nursemaids but God knows what they are up to.'

'There's no time like the present, my friend. Shall we go in search of them?'

* * *

Silchester Court

'Giselle, do we require any more gowns for our sojourn in Bath?' Beth asked.

'I told you, my love, we have sufficient in our wardrobes for every eventuality.' She held up the strange garment they were to wear when they took a dip in the waters. 'Although this covers us from neck to ankle I fear that when wet it will be rather revealing.'

Her cousin giggled. 'I do hope so. I am so looking forward to being considered a fast young lady again. Being well behaved is becoming rather tedious. You didn't know me when I was living with Mary's mama and for that I am glad. I was forever in and out of scrapes and almost eloped with a most unsuitable young man.'

'If you have decided you are now looking for a husband, then you should have gone to London for the Season. I thought we had decided we have no wish to set up our own establishments for another year or two.'

'Fiddlesticks to that! We have exhausted the supply of young gentlemen in this neighbourhood and have found no one who would suit. To be honest, although I love to attend a ball, I didn't like being crushed with strangers. In Bath we can attend the

Assembly Rooms and it will be more enjoyable as there will be fewer people.'

'From what I've heard, there are likely to be more older people than those of similar age to us...'

'I too have done some research into the matter. You are right to say there will be a lot of older folk in Bath who visit to benefit from the waters of the Pump Room, but I'm reliably informed that despite it being less fashionable than it was a few years ago, there are still dozens of families from the *ton* who spend their summers there.'

'If that be the case, Beth, then I am at a loss to understand why Beau agreed so readily to us going without him in attendance.'

'He does not enjoy the constant racket of young people about the place and I believe he will be relieved to see us gone for the summer so he can enjoy Silchester Court in peace.'

'You are right. Much as I love my brother he is not suited to parties and conversation. I don't believe he will ever find himself a bride but will prefer to remain a bachelor living in solitary splendour here after we have all left him.'

'That will be a great shame in my opinion. He is the handsomest of your brothers and must be the most eligible *parti* in the land. Which reminds me, my love, it is high time that you found yourself a suitable husband. You will be considered at your last prayers once you have reached your majority.'

'In which case, Beth, I have a few months to remedy this. However, I have yet to meet a gentleman that I could fall in love with.' She turned away quickly to hide her face. This was not strictly true. There was one gentleman she believed she could easily love if he would only think of her as a woman grown and not a girl just from the schoolroom.

Lord Rushton had known her since she was a child; he was a

contemporary of her brother, which made him twelve years her senior. This difference in ages was not insurmountable, in her opinion, but he was a widower with two daughters and must consider her too immature and inexperienced to become their new mama. That is, of course, if he thought about her at all.

The rain had stopped and the sun was out. 'Come, we can ride now. A gallop will clear our heads.'

Her cousin had not enjoyed this pastime when she had come to live with them last year but with encouragement from herself and her brother, Beth was now an excellent horsewoman and enjoyed careering over the countryside as much as Giselle did.

Beau had gone to visit Lord Rushton at his country estate in Essex and would not return until the morrow. She was eager to know why they had seen so little of his lordship in the past few months and prayed that he wasn't unwell.

* * *

Castlemere

Rushton took his friend up to the schoolroom with some trepidation. Eloise and Estelle were not there and a harassed maid wrung her hands when he asked where his daughters were.

'My lord, I'm not exactly sure. We thought they were playing with their dolls but when we looked they had disappeared. Nancy and Sally have gone to find them.'

Silchester was staring out of the window. 'I can see them; they are hiding in the maze.'

He joined him and couldn't help smiling as he watched them dashing about inside the head-high hedges. 'They are happy children, kind and intelligent, but they have no regard for discipline or obedience.'

'Shall we go and join them? Last time I saw them they were scarcely out of leading strings.'

'That's because, my friend, you rarely come here. I come to Silchester or we meet in Town.'

He led the way through a side door that led directly to the expanse of lawn and down to the maze. For the first time since he could remember he felt a little more optimistic about the future.

The girls couldn't see over the hedges, but as both he and Silchester were more than two yards high the children were visible to them.

'Estelle, Eloise, come out if you please. You have a visitor.'

'Papa, you must come and find us, for I declare that we are quite lost.' Estelle, as the oldest, was usually the first to speak.

'If you found your way to the centre then you are quite capable of finding your way back, young lady. We have no intention of chasing you back and forth in there.'

There was no answer but he knew the girls would come – their natural curiosity to see such an unusual sight as a visitor would bring them out.

Sure enough a few minutes later his daughters emerged. They were both in disarray, their hair ribbons long gone, leaves and dirt on their once white pinafores and their faces and hands in urgent need of a wet cloth.

They were quite unabashed by their disreputable appearance and threw themselves into his arms. He adored both of them; he just wished he was a better parent and that his beloved wife was still there to guide them.

'Papa,' Eloise whispered, 'who is that large gentleman staring at us so particularly?'

He stood up and turned them both to face his friend. 'Your grace, allow me to introduce you to my reprehensible daughters. The one with the dark ringlets is Estelle, the one with the fair curls is Eloise. Make your curtsies, girls.'

Obediently they dipped and Silchester smiled and nodded. 'I'm delighted to meet you. How old might you both be?'

'I am ten years of age, your grace, and my sister, Eloise, is nine years of age.'

'Do you like holidays?'

The girls exchanged bewildered glances. 'I could not say, sir, as I don't think we have ever been on one.' Estelle glanced up at him for confirmation.

'No, sweetheart, you have never been away from Castlemere. Would you like to do so?'

They nodded in unison and waited to be told what was in store for them. Silchester extended the invitation to go to Bath, but neither of his daughters showed any excitement.

This wasn't going to plan. He had expected the girls to be overjoyed at the prospect of spending the summer away from Castlemere. Then he realised they had moved closer to him and were hanging on to his coat-tails. He dropped to his haunches and turned them to face him. 'What is it, little ones? I thought you would be pleased at the prospect.'

Tears were trickling down their cheeks. Eloise buried her face in his shoulder and left her sister to explain. 'We promise we won't be naughty any more, Papa. Please don't send us away; we want to stay with you.'

'This is not a punishment, sweethearts, but a treat. We shall travel together to Silchester Court next week and I shall accompany you. Then, when you are happily acquainted with Lady Giselle and Miss Freemantle you will leave for Bath. The duke and I have business to attend to in Town but will join you after a week or two.'

Silchester had strolled off, leaving him to deal with this domestic crisis on his own. His friend was the best of gentlemen but he was not overly fond of children which, no doubt, explained why he had not set up his own nursery.

'Papa, why are you giving us a reward when we have been so badly behaved that our last three governesses left?' Estelle stared up at him.

'I'm hoping that a change of scene will be enough to persuade you that cooperating with those who are taking care of you is the sensible thing to do.' He looked from one to the other and his expression was stern. 'If you misbehave in any way then you will be returned here and I shall then consider if sending you away to school would be the best option.' The children understood this was to be their last chance at redemption. They both nodded vigorously.

'We will be really, really good, Papa; we shall not let you down,' Estelle said and then grabbed her sister's hand. 'Come along, Ellie, we must go in at once and decide what we are to take with us on this adventure.'

They scampered off, laughing and chattering gaily, and the tightness in his chest began to dissipate. These two were his life and he knew that up until now he had been failing dismally as a parent and their wildness was entirely his fault.

When Silchester departed the following morning arrangements were in place. He was still unsure that presenting the addition of his daughters to the Bath visit as a *fait accompli* was entirely fair on Lady Giselle and her cousin.

He was barely acquainted with Miss Freemantle, but what little he had seen of her last year had been favourable. However, he had known Silchester's sister since she was a child, had watched her develop from an enchanting child to an intelligent and lovely young woman. He was surprised she had not found herself a dashing young husband – so far three of her siblings had fallen in love with and married their partners in rapid succession.

He had attended Lord Aubrey's nuptials last summer, and also the christenings of Lord Sheldon's son and Lady Madeline's daughter in the autumn. Although he had been invited to spend Christmas with them all he had declined the invitation as he had no wish to leave his children over the festive period. Taking them had not been an option either. The thought of visiting Silchester after so long an absence raised his spirits and he was almost as eager to set out as his overexcited daughters.

2

SILCHESTER COURT

Giselle listened to Beau's explanation as to why she and Beth were now going to be obliged to take responsibility for two little girls when they went away for the summer, instead of being able to do as they pleased. She could hardly refuse, especially as Beth was apparently delighted with the news, as to do so would make her seem unsympathetic.

'I think you should have asked us before you made the arrangement. We can hardly refuse when Lord Rushton and his daughters are arriving in a few days.'

'Don't be so uncharitable, Giselle,' Beth told her sternly. 'We will be doing Lord Rushton a favour. Don't forget how much assistance he was to the family last year – it's the very least we can do to show our appreciation.'

Her brother appeared genuinely puzzled by her reaction. 'It didn't occur to me, sweetheart, that you might have any objection to acting as temporary guardians to two delightful children. They have been running poor Rushton ragged these past few months. Some gentlemen are just not cut out to be parents and unfortunately both he and I fall into that category.'

She snorted inelegantly. 'He should have thought of that before he got married and produced his children. You have done the honourable thing by remaining a bachelor.'

'I didn't avoid becoming leg-shackled for that reason. I am a bachelor because I do not believe that I will ever meet anyone I wish to marry.'

'And you have little chance of meeting someone if you remain sequestered here most of the year. You should open the house in Grosvenor Square and see what is on offer this Season. I'm sure there will be a dozen or more young ladies paraded before you.'

'On offer? You make it sound like an auction at Tattersalls. If that's how you think about the Season, I must assume that is why both of you have refused to go this year.'

'Beth and I enjoy dancing as much as any other young lady; what we don't enjoy is being stared at by fortune hunters and other gentlemen searching for a bride. I sometimes think it would be preferable to marry an elderly gentleman who would allow me the freedom to do as I please and keep me safe from predatory males.'

'You are being deliberately outrageous, my girl, and it's fortunate for you that I don't believe one word of what you've just said. I'm sure you *will* meet someone you wish to spend the rest of your life with. After all, we have watched three of our siblings fall neck over crop in love in days of meeting their partners. I believe it to be a family failing.'

'Not a failing, Cousin Beau, I envy all of them for being so happy. I have every intention of finding myself a husband whilst I am in Bath.'

'Good luck with that, my dear. I rather think that Giselle would be more successful in that particular city as she has expressed a preference for an elderly gentleman and there are certainly more of those than any other sort from what I've heard.'

* * *

That night Giselle was unable to sleep. Her head was full of images of Lord Rushton. A man of his age could be considered past his prime, but in her opinion he was the epitome of everything a gentleman should be. He was slightly taller than Beau, had striking green eyes – and if she was to criticise anything, it would be his hair colour. This was neither fair nor dark but something in between.

Until Beau had told her the sad story of Lady Rushton's demise from a congestion of the lungs, she had not truly understood his circumstances. To have married so young to his childhood sweetheart and then to lose her so tragically made him seem like a figure from a romance. She had met him dozens of times, found him entertaining company but had never considered him a grieving widow, or a delinquent father.

In fact, if she was honest, she had thought of him as a bachelor – the contemporary of her older brother and, like him, too set in his ways to wish to give up his single state. She could not imagine Beau falling in love as Aubrey and Bennett had done – he was not given to such romantical fancies. If he ever married, it would be for pragmatic reasons.

When she conjured up the face of the gentleman she intended to fall in love with, more often than not, it was Rushton's face that intruded on her dreams. Now she viewed him differently. She would put him out of her thoughts. She had no intention of competing with the spectre of his wife. She smiled in the darkness and came to a decision. Like Beth she was determined to find the man she wished to marry during her sojourn at Bath.

One thing she was sure of: having the two little girls was going to make things more difficult. The duke and Rushton would be joining them after a week or two. Therefore, being responsible for Estelle and Eloise should not prove too much of a handicap in her search for a husband. She loved children and had no intention of being anything but a loving and responsible guardian to them for the short time they were to be in her charge.

As she was eventually drifting off to sleep it occurred to her that it was strange Lord Rushton had been part of her family circle ever since she could remember, but she had never met the children or his long-departed wife.

* * *

Castlemere

The carriage with the baggage had departed hours ago but Rushton was still awaiting the long-delayed arrival of his two daughters and their nursemaid. It was an arduous journey to Hertfordshire and if they didn't set off in the next half an hour they would be obliged to overnight a third time somewhere *en route*.

This was unacceptable behaviour and not a good start to this expedition. He took the stairs two at a time and arrived on the nursery floor to hear one of his girls sobbing noisily. What now? He threw open the schoolroom door to see Eloise in a heap on the floor – there was no sign of her sister.

'Sweetheart, what is wrong? Why are you making such a racket?' He reached down and hoisted her into his arms. She didn't stop crying, just pressed her tear-streaked face to his immaculate stock. 'Where is your sister? Where is the nursemaid?'

The child gulped, shuddered and managed to tell him what was wrong. 'Estelle has run away. She doesn't want to go to Bath with Lady Giselle – she doesn't want to go anywhere unless you come with us.'

He removed the handkerchief from his waistcoat pocket, stood her on a nearby chair, and wiped her face clean. 'I'm sure she hasn't gone very far, little one. We shall find her together. I assume that the nursemaid has gone in search of your sister?'

'She has, Papa, but Estelle told me she would stay hidden until it was too late for us to leave. Then Lady Giselle would go to Bath without us and we will all stay here as usual.'

'Do you wish to go or are you of the same mind as your sister?'

'I do want to go. I think it will be such fun. Much better than staying here.'

'Then, we shall leave your sister behind. She is quite right to say that any further delay will mean you will miss your opportunity. Therefore, Estelle must remain here on her own and you shall have a wonderful time without her.'

He had been speaking loudly, knowing that his daughter would be hiding somewhere close by. He wasn't going to be drawn into her schemes; he meant what he said. However, he was hoping common sense would prevail, and the child would emerge when she understood she couldn't dictate matters by her bad behaviour.

Eloise looked stricken but he winked at her and smiled and she understood immediately. 'I don't mind if she stays behind as long as I can go. Shall we leave at once, Papa? The carriage has been outside this age and the horses will be too tired to travel all that distance if they are left to stand about much longer.'

When had his youngest child begun to sound like a woman twice her age? He had been in residence with them these past ten months but had obviously not got to know them as a good father should.

With Eloise's hand in his he gently led her out of the room. They had reached the front door before the missing child hurtled down the stairs and threw herself against him.

'Please, Papa, don't leave me behind. I do want to come, I do, I do. I was just being silly.'

He gripped her firmly on the shoulder and turned her so she was facing him. 'Your behaviour has been disappointing, young lady, and I give you fair warning that if anything like this occurs a second time you will indeed be left here on your own all summer.'

She stiffened beneath his touch and for a horrible moment he thought she might snatch herself away and rush off again. Then she nodded, but her head was lowered so he couldn't see her expression. 'I give you my word, Papa. I will be the best-behaved child in the kingdom from now on.'

The flustered nursemaid arrived at a run and curtsied. 'I beg your pardon, my lord, we are ready to depart now and I apologise for keeping you waiting.'

It was hardly the girl's fault, but he wasn't going to get into a discussion with the servant. He released both children, and the maid took a firm grip of their hands and escorted them briskly to the carriage. They were to travel in the interior but he was going to ride. There was nothing he disliked more than being cooped up in a stuffy coach for hours. His valet was already sitting inside, none too happy about the delay.

He travelled across the fields, jumping the hedges and ditches as he came to them, but was reunited with the carriage at midday at a respectable hostelry where his man of business had already bespoken a cold collation to be served in a private parlour.

Both girls were in good humour and there was no mention of the incident that had almost made them tardy. 'You have another half an hour to stretch your legs and use the facilities, girls, but then you must return to the coach without delay. We should be at Silchester by noon the day after tomorrow – they will be expecting us.'

'Will we be departing as soon as we arrive?'

'No, Estelle, you will be leaving at first light the following day. We are stopping in St Albans tomorrow night and if you are not too tired I shall take you to see the Roman ruins.'

The journey progressed as planned with no further interruptions or histrionics from his daughters. He had decided to take it slowly so he would not be obliged to change horses and endure all the inconvenience that involved.

He cantered ahead of the carriage when he turned through the imposing gateway that led onto the Silchester estate. His approach had been observed and there was a groom waiting to take his stallion when he dismounted.

'You have made better time than I expected, my friend. Is the carriage far behind you?' Silchester said as he came out to greet him.

'Not far; did the luggage arrive safely?'

'It came this morning. The trunks are now safely installed with those of my sister and cousin. Everything is ready for their departure at dawn tomorrow. Come in. My sister and cousin are eager to become reacquainted with you.'

***

Silchester Court

Giselle had spent the morning with her sister Madeline. Grey, Lord Carshalton, had been overseeing his estates, allowing them to interact with baby Eleanor alone.

'I can't believe how much she has grown in the past few months. She will be walking before she is a year old if she continues to heave herself up on the edge of the sofa as she is doing,' she said to her sister.

'Grace and Bennett's son, Richard, is crawling everywhere, but my daughter seems to have missed out that step in her development.' The baby lost her grip and tumbled backwards onto the carpet. Instead of screaming at this mishap, she laughed and rolled over onto her tummy and pushed herself upright again.

'She is so like you. No one would ever mistake her for anyone but a member of the Sheldon family.'

'Richard is the image of Bennett. He is now in line for the dukedom as Beau shows no sign of wishing to be married.'

'I don't think he enjoys the company of children, which is why we have never met Lord Rushton's daughters before now. I've had little experience of them myself. I cannot imagine why our brother took it upon himself to volunteer Beth and I to take care of these little girls all summer.'

'Can you not? It is as plain as the nose on your face, my love. He had no wish to refuse permission for you to go to Bath, but equally he has no wish for you to be gadding about the place making unsuitable connections in his absence. Having the two little girls in tow will keep you out of trouble – at least that's what I think he believes.'

Giselle laughed. 'I have a nasty feeling I will be the one acting in *loco parentis* as Beth has decided she will not come back to Silchester without having become betrothed. Our cousin is bound to get into mischief, especially as there will be no one in authority to prevent her doing so. She has already told me she has no intention of being involved with the girls – that they are my responsibility as I am the oldest by two years.'

'I sincerely hope, my dear, that you have not told our brother what Beth is planning. He would refuse to let either of you go and the children would be so disappointed. Mind you, I cannot see that there is much to entertain children of that age – they will hardly wish to take the waters and are too young to attend the nightly assemblies.'

'I believe there are several historical places of interest nearby, also the recently built Theatre Royal and the Royal Crescent and Assembly Rooms are supposed to be magnificent. We shall go for drives in the country in an open carriage, promenade in the Pump Room and visit the circulating libraries.'

'I cannot see any of that being of interest to nine- and ten-year-olds. Perhaps there will be other families with children of a similar age that you can introduce them to.'

'I sincerely hope so, for the more we talk about it the less I am looking forward to the experience. I must go. They are expected late this morning and I must be there to greet them.'

Giselle had ridden over and her mare was waiting for her when she emerged at the front of the house. She did not bother to have a groom accompany her on so short a ride, but did require assistance to mount.

In the three hours she had spent with her sister one name had not been mentioned – they had talked about everyone else, but not Lord Rushton. She had only discovered last night that

An Accommodating Husband

his given name was Henry – he didn't look like a Henry – but even in her innermost thoughts she could not be so presumptuous as to think of him as anything but Lord Rushton.

Her heart sunk to her boots when she arrived in the stable yard to find not only Lord Rushton's horse safely installed in a stable, but also his carriage in the coach house. She was appallingly tardy. Should she go in and greet the arrivals as she was, or return to her apartment and change into something more suitable than her riding habit?

As she was already late it could hardly matter if she was even later, and she was certain her brother would not take kindly to her appearing in her dirt. Her maid, Jenny, had a sprig muslin gown ready waiting.

'Oh, my lady, you were sent for an age ago. Quickly, let me help you wash the smell of horse from your person and then you can step into your gown. Fortunately, your hair needs little attention.'

'How long ago did Lord Rushton arrive?'

'An hour ago, and his daughters came shortly afterwards.'

As soon as she was respectable Giselle picked up her skirts and dashed through the house in a most unbecoming way. As she tore past the staircase that led to the nursery floor, two little faces peeped around the corner at her.

She skidded to a stop. 'You must be Estelle and Eloise. I beg your pardon for being so late – I shall come up immediately to further our acquaintance, but first I must make grovelling apologies to your papa.' She smiled at them. 'I promise you I'm not usually unpunctual.'

The dark-haired child curtsied. 'I think the duke is very cross with you, Lady Giselle. Where have you been?'

'I have been visiting with my sister, but I must not dally here and make things worse.' With a wave of her hand she continued her precipitous progress and only slowed as she approached the open doors to the grand drawing room.

As she was about to step in, someone spoke from behind her. So startled was she that she lost her balance and put her foot through the hem of her gown.

3

SILCHESTER COURT

Rushton had been about to ascend the stairs in order to fetch his daughters so that they might be introduced when he heard someone running along the passageway upstairs. He didn't deliberately move into the shadows, but was curious as to who might be breaking all the rules of decorum in this way.

There was the sound of someone talking and he realised it was the missing Lady Giselle. Silchester was fuming that his sister had not been there to make her curtsy but Rushton had been agreeably entertained by Miss Freemantle in her absence.

The girl was quite enchanting, as charming as she was beautiful. Blue eyes and golden curls were not to his taste; he preferred women with dark hair and eyes as they reminded him of his lost love. Fortunately, neither of his daughters had inherited his own mouse-brown locks.

Lady Giselle hurtled down the stairs with more speed than dignity and he stepped forward to warn her Silchester was on the warpath.

'Lady Giselle...'

The girl stumbled and there was an ominous tearing sound.

'That was poorly done of you, sir. I have now ruined a new gown. Did nobody ever tell you that to leap out at a person is bad manners?'

He had been about to apologise but he objected to being spoken to so impertinently. 'You have only yourself to blame, my lady. If you had not been running—'

She interrupted him for a second time. 'I was running, my lord, because I was late and had kept you waiting an unconscionable time. Now, as you can see, I must return to my apartment again in order to change into something that is not torn.'

Her eyes flashed and there was a hectic colour staining her cheeks. He was about to tell her in no uncertain terms exactly what he thought when Silchester appeared in the doorway. He raised an aristocratic eyebrow.

'Good grief, Giselle, not only are you late but you are also in disarray.'

Rushton thought the girl would stamp her foot. Instead he heard her take a deep breath and then step away from her brother.

'I am well aware that I cannot come in as I am. I suggest that you ask why it is I'm in this state as it is entirely Rushton's doing.' She said no more, but turned and ran lightly up the stairs before either of them could remonstrate with her.

Silchester chuckled. 'I must apologise for my rag-mannered sister, my friend; she is usually impeccably behaved. To what was she referring? How are you to blame for her appearance?'

'I startled her and she put her foot through her gown so I suppose I could be said to have caused the accident. I do not remember her being so outspoken – I'm beginning to regret my decision to send my girls to Bath with her. If this is how she behaves, then she will not set a good example to my daughters.'

An Accommodating Husband

This was a bad move on his part as the duke did not take criticism of his family lightly.

'I think, Rushton, that your girls are so badly behaved any example set before them will be a good one.'

The matter hung in the balance for a second and then they both laughed. 'I've no wish to be at odds with you. I apologise for—'

'No need, my friend, I am too quick to take offence when none is intended; and you are right to say that Giselle behaved quite out of character just now. She is rarely late for an appointment and is always sweet-natured and conciliatory. She was none of those things this morning.'

'I'm going to fetch my girls – they must make their curtsies to you all. I sincerely hope that they will be on their best behaviour today or it will be Miss Freemantle and your sister who call quits on the arrangement.'

He found his daughters sitting on the bottom step of the staircase that led to the upper floor. 'Papa, we like Lady Giselle. Are we to come down and meet the duke and Miss Freemantle now?'

'Indeed you are, Estelle. You must comport yourselves well. I'm sure you don't wish to be obliged to return to Castlemere after having come so far.' There was no need for him to say more; they understood exactly what he meant.

He ushered them in front of him and they walked demurely down the stairs, hand in hand, the epitome of good behaviour. Seeing them as they were, no one would have believed they were the worst-behaved children he had ever met.

He bit back a laugh at his ridiculous thought. As he knew no other children he had no idea if his summation of the situation was correct. However, he was quite certain children were better seen and not heard, and that they should do as they were told without quibbling. On both counts his girls failed miserably.

Their introduction into society went well and he could not fault their manners. When Lady Giselle eventually joined them they gravitated to her side immediately. Within a short space of time the three of them were playing a lively game of spillikins. It did not go unnoticed by either himself or his host that Miss Freemantle made no effort to join them and preferred to remain with the adults.

When the children became too noisy a quiet word from her ladyship was enough to restore order. How was it that this young girl, scarcely out of the schoolroom as far as he was concerned, could do so easily what he could not?

* * *

The baggage departed, along with the two nursemaids and both personal maids, several hours before the carriage in which Giselle, her cousin and the two girls were to travel. Again, they were to take the journey in two easy stages, overnighting at a town called Swindon and hopefully arriving mid-afternoon at their destination in Queen Square. This, she had reliably been informed, was exactly the place to reside, as from there they could easily walk to the Theatre Royal, the Assembly Rooms and the Pump Room.

When it was their turn to leave, the girls scampered out and scrambled into the carriage without a second thought. Beth sailed across the turning circle, eager to be on her way. Giselle found herself reluctant to begin this excursion. The idea had been her cousin's. She had gone along with it believing a few months away from Silchester would be beneficial, not only for

Beth, but also for her brother who was becoming disgruntled by the constant stream of noisy visitors.

* * *

They had an uneventful journey to the inn at which they were going to spend the night, but they were all glad to be out of the carriage. The girls had proved to be entertaining companions and even Beth had begun to take an interest in them.

'We will have to manage for ourselves tonight, but I'm sure that will not be a problem, will it?' Giselle fixed both children with a firm look.

'We promised Papa we would behave ourselves and we always keep our promises, don't we, Eloise?'

'We do, Aunt Giselle, and we don't want to be sent home early in disgrace.'

Lord Rushton had insisted that his daughters referred to both she and Beth as their aunt – this made her feel decidedly old and she should much prefer to be called by her given name.

'Then I suggest that we stretch our legs by walking around the town for half an hour. After that we shall return and find our accommodation. Mr Carstairs, the duke's man of business, has made all the arrangements in advance so I'm certain everything will be in order.'

There was not a great deal to see but she enjoyed the fresh air and exercise. 'I do hope that there will be suitable riding horses for us when we arrive tomorrow. I know that there is a barouche available to us, but it would be more enjoyable to ride.'

'We cannot take our charges with us when on horseback, Giselle, so I fear we will be constrained to use the carriage.'

'Good heavens! I have no intention of spending every minute

with the girls – they have their nursemaids and there should be a new governess appointed as well. We shall take them out in the afternoons, and that will suffice.'

'Look at that. There must be an army barracks close by. I love to see an officer in his regimentals, do not you?'

'I'm not so enamoured of a man in uniform as yourself, my dear. My brother Bennett was a major and now I have another brother, Perry, acting as an intelligence officer in Spain. Madeline's husband was also an officer before he resigned his commission. So, you can understand that a gentleman in a uniform only serves to remind me of the dangers my brother is in.'

Beth giggled. 'But you must own, they are prodigiously handsome and the horses they are riding are quite magnificent. The blue of the Hussars is more attractive, in my opinion, than the red worn by the infantry.'

The children, attracted by their comments, pointed at the two officers. 'See, they are turning into the inn yard. We shall be able to...'

'Enough, girls, it is impolite to point. Those cavalry officers are none of our concern and you will keep your comments to yourself, if you please.'

Suitably subdued, the girls apologised prettily, and skipped ahead hand in hand. They looked angelic, but she was not fooled for a minute. She knew, from what Beau had told her, that they could be difficult. Hopefully the threat of being returned prematurely would be enough to keep them in line.

The landlord was expecting them and sent not one, but two maids to escort them to their chambers. They had an elegant suite of rooms at the rear of the building. There were two bedchambers and a private sitting room – perfect for their requirements.

An Accommodating Husband

'You will sleep in here, girls, and we shall be next door. You are quite old enough to unpack your night things and other necessities, are you not?' She gestured to the small boxes standing at the foot of the bed.

The girls agreed that they could do this task without supervision and Giselle left them exclaiming and giggling with excitement.

'It is fortunate indeed, Beth, that this bed is so commodious, as neither of us are accustomed to sharing.'

'I left my reticule in the carriage, Giselle. I shall run down and get it. I shall not be above a few minutes.'

Before she could tell her cousin to send a maid on this errand the girl had vanished with a whisk of her skirts. She was about to go after her when the children demanded her attention.

'We can see right across the fields from our window, Aunt Giselle. There are cows in the nearest one. May we open the window and see if we are able to hear them lowing?' Eloise asked.

'You can have the window open for now, but I suggest that you close it before you retire, otherwise you might be woken at dawn by the animals out there.'

By the time she had assisted them with their request the hot water had arrived and she was informed by the maids that the supper trays would be arriving shortly.

Where was her cousin? Surely it did not take above ten minutes to find somebody to fetch her reticule? She could hardly abandon her charges in order to go and find Beth, but she had a nasty suspicion it wasn't her reticule that the girl had gone in search of.

Sure enough – she discovered her cousin was outside in the yard flirting outrageously with one of the cavalry officers. This was a side to Beth she had never seen; indeed, since she had come to live with them at Silchester Court the girl had been an exemplary member of the family. However, this was the first time Beth did not have to answer to either of her brothers.

Giselle wasn't sure if it would be best to interrupt the conversation herself or send one of the gawping stable boys with a message. As she hesitated the matter was resolved for her. The second officer, obviously of a senior rank to the other, interrupted the *tête-à-tête*. The one that Beth had been talking to bowed and marched smartly away to remount his horse.

Hastily Giselle returned to their chambers, not wishing to be seen lurking on the stairs. She hoped that her cousin would mention this breach of etiquette on her part, so would not speak of what she had seen and wait to see how her cousin behaved on her return.

'See, I have it.' Beth waved her reticule in the air triumphantly. 'The trays have come. I am quite hungry and hope the food tastes as good as it smells.'

A cloth had been put across the polished wooden table, cutlery and glassware laid up, and four chairs placed around it. There were a variety of dishes on the sideboard and it would appear they were to help themselves as the maids were no longer there.

It wasn't until the girls were asleep that she had the opportunity to mention to Beth what she had seen. 'I am disappointed that you didn't see fit to tell me you had introduced yourself to one of those cavalry officers. That was poorly done of you, Beth; you should not have been anywhere near either of them without a chaperone. And even then, it is not done to speak to a gentleman one hasn't been introduced to.'

'Fiddlesticks to that! For the first time in over a year I can do as I please – you must be so relieved not to have the duke watching every move you make. I told you we would have fun this summer and I believe that it has already started.'

Giselle swallowed a lump in her throat. 'So that is why you suggested we spend the summer in Bath. You have deceived us all as to your true character. I shall write at once to Beau and tell him he must join us immediately, as you are determined to ruin your reputation.'

Beth's sunny smile vanished. She jumped to her feet and rushed over to throw her arms around Giselle. 'No, no, you misunderstand me, dearest friend. The lieutenant was kind enough to fetch my reticule when I couldn't find a groom to do so for me. He was perfectly polite. I did not overstep the mark at any time, and I promise you nothing untoward took place apart from me thanking him for his help.'

'I saw you together so you cannot lie to me. I might not be experienced in the ways of the world, but I do know when a young lady is flirting with a gentleman.'

Beth had the grace to blush. 'I couldn't help myself. He made me feel like the heroine of one of my romances. I don't even know his name and he certainly doesn't know mine. I have not deceived you; I have always been of a lively character...'

'I understand that, but what you just said is hardly reassuring. I have the two girls' welfare to consider and now it would seem I must monitor your behaviour too if we are not to be disgraced.'

'I beg your pardon. I give you my solemn promise I shall do nothing to bring disrepute to the family. I didn't mean what I said about doing as I please because Cousin Beau is not here to reprimand me.' She folded her stockinged feet under her and sat down. 'I love my cousin, but he is rather austere and tends to look down his nose at one at the slightest infringement of his very high standards. Surely you will feel more relaxed when he is not frowning at us for making too much noise with our friends and acquaintances when they come to visit?'

She was forced to smile. 'He can be a tad disapproving, but he is a wonderful brother and head of the family. I accept your apology and your promise not to breach the rules of etiquette again. Now, I think we should retire as we are to leave at first light.'

* * *

The house in Queen Square lived up to expectations. It was not, of course, anything near as grand as the house in Grosvenor Square, but nevertheless it was substantial and more than adequate for their summer visit.

The only drawback that Giselle could see was the fact that the garden was not as large as she'd hoped. There was a pleasant flagged terrace, with steps leading down to the lawn, and this could be accessed through double doors from the drawing room. The house possessed its own coach house, stabling and accommodation for the grooms, as well as a laundry directly behind the kitchen.

They were greeted by the housekeeper, Ashworth, and the butler, Simpson, and a row of smartly dressed maids and two liveried footmen. More than adequate for so small a household.

'This will do very well, will it not, Beth? The furnishings are new and the chambers spacious.'

'It is quite perfect. Shall I take the girls up for you? I think that must be the new governess waiting to speak with you.'

Her cousin vanished with the children and Giselle turned to greet the tall, thin, unsmiling woman dressed entirely in black.

4

BATH

Giselle remained where she was and let the woman approach. She raised an eyebrow but said nothing. The governess reluctantly curtsied.

'I am Miss Gibbons, your ladyship. Mr Carstairs appointed me to take care of Lord Rushton's daughters whilst they are here.'

'You are to attend to their schoolwork in the mornings but will have many afternoons free, as Miss Freemantle and I intend to take the girls out with us.'

She had expected Miss Gibbons to object, to look even more grim if that were possible. To her astonishment, the woman's demeanour changed and she smiled, making her look almost pretty.

'Several afternoons? In my previous employment I was fortunate indeed to get a day off a month. I cannot say how delighted I am to be working here. I thought I would concentrate on the basics – reading, writing and arithmetic – but I am happy to add music, deportment and watercolours to their curriculum if you would like me to.'

'Please, Miss Gibbons, shall we go somewhere more comfortable to talk?' She gestured to a hovering footman. 'Have refreshments sent to the drawing room and please send a message to the nursery that the girls are to come down and meet their governess.'

Once they were seated, Giselle smiled at her companion. 'Forgive me for asking, but are you in mourning?'

'I am not, my lady. My previous employers preferred me to dress sombrely.'

'Well, whilst you are here I wish you to wear something more cheerful. I'm sure there is a seamstress nearby who could make you fresh gowns. It will be at our expense of course.'

'That will not be necessary, my lady. I have several suitable items in my wardrobe. I thank you for your generosity.'

There was no time to say more as Estelle and Eloise rushed in – there was no sign of her cousin. Giselle glanced sideways to see how the governess reacted to the boisterous arrival of her charges.

'Good afternoon, girls, I am to be your teacher whilst you are in Bath. I am Miss Gibbons.' She patted the spaces on either side of her on the *chaise longue*. 'I'm surprised to see you both so energetic after travelling so far.'

Estelle sat down first. 'I fear that we are always lively, Miss Gibbons. We both find it hard to be quiet and walk slowly.'

'I'm delighted to hear you say so, my dear; I cannot abide an inactive child.' She smiled encouragingly at Eloise and the little girl moved forward and took her place. 'There is a pretty garden, children. We must go and explore it after we have partaken of this delicious spread.'

After consuming several scones with strawberry preserve, and drinking a large glass of freshly squeezed lemonade, the girls were ready to depart. Miss Gibbons brushed the crumbs from her skirts and looked enquiringly in her direction.

'Would it be in order for me to take the girls outside?'

'Of course it would, as obviously this afternoon I will not be going anywhere.' Giselle was concerned that Beth had not appeared and was about to go in search of her when her cousin arrived.

'Good, I'm glad you have left some scones for me. I apologise for being tardy. I had to write a letter and get a footman to post it for me.'

'The new governess is ideal and the girls appear to have taken to her immediately. I'm beginning to think our visit to Bath will be more pleasurable than I at first thought.'

'She looked like a dragon, but I will take your word that she is better than her appearance might indicate.'

'I am going to change into a fresh ensemble. I see that you have done so already, Beth. Then, as Miss Gibbons has the girls in hand, I thought we might stroll to the Pump Room and perhaps visit the circulating library.'

* * *

Bath was everything she had hoped and when Beth saw a notice for a dance to be held at the Assembly Rooms the following evening she was thrilled.

'We must go, Giselle. It is why we came here, after all.'

'Mr Carstairs will arrive here tomorrow morning and he will explain how things are done here. I'm not sure it will be acceptable to attend when we know nobody there – especially as we don't have a gentleman to escort us. And, for your information, Beth, it is you who is in the hope of meeting your future husband, not I.'

* * *

Her bedchamber was, like the rest of the house, well appointed. Although not as substantial as the one she had at home, it was more than adequate for a summer visit. Carstairs was to speak to them at ten o'clock so she would have to postpone her ride until after that. She could not wait to try out the pretty bay mare that had been purchased for her.

Beth had said she was going to explore the emporiums the following morning so did not intend to accompany her. Giselle intended to ask Carstairs if it was within the bounds of propriety for Beth to gallivant about the place with just her personal maid in attendance.

Jenny had put out her riding habit – it hardly seemed sensible to put on a morning gown and then change after an hour or so. Miss Gibbons had refused to join them for dinner saying it wasn't her place, but if they had a supper party she would be happy to make up the numbers if necessary.

There was no sign of her cousin in the breakfast room and when she enquired she was told Beth had asked for a tray to be sent to her bedchamber. The girls, naturally, would eat in their own domain upstairs.

There was far too much on the sideboard for one person, but she supposed the staff would make sure nothing went to waste. She ate little – for some reason she was on edge today and she couldn't think why.

When Beau's man of business appeared she was waiting for him in the library. This seemed a more appropriate place for their discussion than the drawing room.

She put her concerns to him and he was able to reassure her. 'Miss Freemantle is not offending anyone by visiting the shops, my lady. As long as she has her maid with her at all times, that is. As to attending the ball this evening, I had anticipated you wishing to go and have already taken out a subscription for both of you. A Mrs Forsyth will call this afternoon and she will be your sponsor.

'She is married to the richest man in Somerset, and is much respected here. She launched her own daughters successfully without taking them to London and believes she will find you and Miss Freemantle suitable husbands too.'

'Good heavens! I hope that doesn't mean we will be introduced to a string of hopeful young gentlemen. It is to escape such people that I came here.' She smiled and continued. 'However, Mrs Forsyth is welcome to find Beth a husband, as my cousin is determined not to return to Silchester without a betrothal ring on her finger.'

Giselle returned from an enjoyable exploration of the surrounding countryside to discover that her cousin was still absent. She sent for the butler. 'Has there been no word from Miss Freemantle?'

'No, my lady, nothing. I have taken the liberty of sending the footmen in search of her as it is possible she has become lost and not able to find her way back. I apologise for not sending one of them with her when she went, but she insisted she had no need.'

'Thank you, Simpson.'

After completing her ablutions and stepping into a pretty sprigged muslin gown Giselle had the remainder of the morning to herself. She decided to explore the outside as she was now familiar with the interior of the substantial building.

It wasn't until shortly after midday that her errant cousin eventually returned to the house. She was apologetic, but not unduly so. 'I met the most interesting people at the Pump Room and will introduce you tonight when we go to the Assembly Rooms.'

'That's all very well, Beth, but you can't disappear like that again. I have been beside myself with worry, and Simpson sent out the footmen to look for you. They visited the Pump Room and said they did not see you.'

'I was not there the whole time. Anyway, I am back now and will join you for a midday repast. Did you enjoy your ride?'

'Do not try and fob me off with questions about my activities, Elizabeth, it is what you have been doing all morning that concerns me.'

'Oh dear! Are you to behave like Mary in future? When I was in her care she always called me Elizabeth if she was displeased.'

'I came here believing it would be the girls I would have to watch carefully, but it seems it is you that is likely to cause me distress by your behaviour.'

'I told you why I have come here, dearest Giselle, I wish to be married. Our intention is to stay here until July, but I doubt any eligible gentlemen will remain as long, so I have only a few weeks to achieve my objective.'

There was little point in continuing this discussion, for this was a young lady she didn't recognise – her cousin was three years from her majority and could not marry without Beau's consent. Therefore, it was not her responsibility to keep Beth from disaster. She would do her best to persuade the girl she had come to love like a sister to act with discretion, but as she was still a minor herself she had no real authority over anyone.

'Did you know that there are weekly concerts at the Upper Assembly Rooms on Wednesdays? We must attend those as well as the balls.' She smiled at her cousin. 'The Theatre Royal boasts shows as good as any one might see in Town – I'm hoping there might be something suitable for the girls to see.'

'As you know, Giselle, I am not overfond of music, but I shall accompany you willingly if you will come with me to every ball. I have never attended a play and think I would enjoy seeing one whilst I am here.'

'Then we are agreed. We are to have morning callers this afternoon. Carstairs has had cards sent out announcing we are here. There is one other thing I wish to discuss with you. Knowing my brother as I do, I cannot fathom why he gave his permission for us to come here without supervision. Do you have any notion why he might have allowed this?'

'I must own that I was surprised when he agreed to our suggestion. I think that Mr Carstairs is acting on his behalf – after all he is in residence here too, is he not?'

'Yes, he has an apartment somewhere which is part of this building but does not have a direct access. Surely you understand that only a member of the family can reside with unmarried ladies without causing comment?'

This news appeared to please Beth. 'Then we are free to come and go without the necessity of asking his permission...'

'My brother trusted both of us to behave with decorum and not bring the family name into disrepute. I hope he was correct in that assumption?'

Beth jumped to her feet without answering this question. 'If we are to have callers in an hour or so I had better do something about my appearance.'

She was gone before Giselle could obtain an answer. She heard Miss Gibbons and the girls in the hall outside the door and went out to speak to them. They assured her that they were having an excellent time and were to walk down to the Pump Room and try the waters for themselves.

'I don't expect it will taste very nice, Aunt Giselle, but our governess said we must try something new every day,' Estelle said.

'Then I shall do so too, but not today. I thought to take you out in the carriage tomorrow afternoon, to Bristol, where we might visit Blaise Castle as it is only a short drive away.'

'Can Miss Gibbons come too?' Eloise asked.

'Would you like to accompany us, Miss Gibbons? The afternoon is yours to do as you please but I should be glad of the company as I doubt that Miss Freemantle will wish to come.'

'I should love to take a carriage ride with you, my lady. I have had few opportunities to do this.'

The governess shepherded the children outside, leaving Giselle to her thoughts. Perhaps it would be wise to write to her brother and invite him to join them at his earliest convenience.

5

It hardly seemed worthwhile getting the carriage out for so short a journey, so Giselle decided it would be sensible to walk to the Assembly Rooms. Carstairs was to accompany them, also their maids carrying their dancing slippers, and a footman to carry a flambeau to light them home. As they were on foot they had both chosen gowns that wouldn't make this difficult.

Beth twirled, sending the diaphanous material of her gown flying out and revealing her trim ankles, silk stockings and petticoats. 'I am so excited. Even though we had half a Season in London I have not attended that many dances.'

'I thought that you were a regular visitor to the Assembly Rooms when you were living in Somerset with Mary and her mama.'

'I did, but they don't count as there were no interesting gentlemen for me to dance with. It is decidedly odd wearing boots with this ensemble. Are you sure we cannot go in the carriage?'

'Quite certain, my love. Mrs Forsyth assured me that only

those who live on the outskirts of the city come in a carriage. Everybody else walks as Bath is so small.'

'Excuse me, my lady, I wish to put on your cloak,' Jenny said.

Giselle waited for her maid to finish and then their small party was ready. Carstairs looked smart in his evening rig and one would have mistaken him for a wealthy gentleman if one didn't know better.

They had not travelled more than a few yards when another family emerged from their house on the square and soon she and Beth were part of a cavalcade of gentry, all dressed for a ball, heading towards the Assembly Rooms.

Each group walked alone. There was no attempt to mingle or hold a conversation. They arrived at their destination along with dozens of others and it was a sad crush in the ladies' retiring rooms. Once she and Beth had changed into the correct footwear, and had the ribbons of their matching fans slipped over their wrists, they were ready to join the throng.

Mr Carstairs ushered them through the press of people and towards Mrs Forsyth who was holding court in the most desirable position in the ballroom. Giselle was the only member of the aristocracy present and she was uncomfortable with all the curtsying she received.

'My dear Lady Giselle, Miss Freemantle, the dancing is about to start. There are a few eager gentlemen waiting to be introduced, so I suggest you cast your eye over them and tell me which of those you would like me to beckon forward.'

'I shall leave the decision to you, ma'am. As long as you select someone who will not tread on my toes, I shall be satisfied.' Giselle turned speak to Beth but her cousin was no longer at her side. There was no time for her to go in search of her as she was introduced to a lanky young man with a shock of black hair and a lopsided smile.

He led her onto the floor and he was a lively partner. 'I thank you, sir – that was most enjoyable.' He escorted her back to Mrs Forsyth then went in search of another willing young lady. Giselle was about to ask the matron if she had seen her cousin when the distinctive uniform of an officer in the Hussars caught her eye. Surely this could not be a coincidence?

Then her worst fears were realised as Beth appeared at his side. Immediately he bowed and, with her hand on his sleeve, he led her forward to dance.

'My word, would you look at that. I can't recall seeing such a thing before. The officer is obviously an acquaintance of Miss Freemantle – such a handsome gentleman – although I find the wearing of the jacket over one shoulder rather unusual,' Mrs Forsyth gushed. 'One would have thought it impossible to promenade around the floor dressed as he is. I do declare that his white breeches and boots set off the dark blue uniform to perfection, do not you think, Lady Giselle?'

All Giselle could think was that Beth had invited this young officer to follow her to Bath. She had been roundly deceived by her cousin and could only see this liaison ending in disaster for both parties. The nameless officer could well be absent without leave – although, after reconsideration, this was unlikely as he would hardly have appeared in his full regimentals in so public a place if he was wanted as a deserter. She could not interrupt the dance but was determined to accost them both as soon as it ended.

The music played interminably and with each turn, skip, bow and curtsy that Beth and her partner made, Giselle became angrier. It hardly seemed credible the young lady looking so angelic on the dance floor was, in fact, a teller of the most awful falsehoods.

The only comfort one could take from this spectacle was

that she had already sent a letter by express to Beau, which he should receive this evening. If he left at first light he could be with them the following day. She prayed this would be in time to stop Beth from doing something irretrievable.

* * *

As the young officer was the only military gentleman present he was much in demand once he had finished his dance with Beth. This gave Giselle the opportunity to corner her cousin and speak her mind.

'Are you so beyond the pale, Elizabeth, that you do not even introduce your dance partner to me? Who is he and how does he come to be here when you gave me your solemn vow you had done no more than exchange pleasantries when you met a few days ago?'

'I promise you, Giselle, I didn't even give him my name. However, he must have enquired from one of our grooms as to our destination. He has a month's furlough before being posted to join his regiment abroad and so decided to follow me here. Don't you think that is the most romantic thing in the world?'

'I think it quite scandalous. I take it you were with him this morning when you were supposed to be viewing the emporiums?'

'I was in the Pump Room when he sent me a note. His name is Theodore Sullivan and he is the son of one Colonel Sullivan, retired. He is an only child and stands to inherit a reasonable fortune when his father dies. They are a military family and although he would have preferred another profession, he had no choice but to become a soldier.'

'That's all very well, but why didn't you bring him across and introduce him before you took to the dance floor in front of the most prestigious families in the city?'

'I apologise, I should have done so, but I was so pleased to see him I quite forgot. I have told him to make his bow as soon as he has finished dancing with his current partner.'

With this Giselle had to be satisfied. She still thought it odd that the young man had pursued Beth in this way, and she was glad she had sent for her brother. He would know exactly what to do and would send the rogue packing if he was in any way unsuitable to be an acquaintance of the family.

When he came to introduce himself she was pleasantly surprised. Not only was he a handsome young man, he appeared well-mannered and did not give the impression of being a fortune hunter. Whilst her cousin was dancing with another partner he led her onto the floor.

'Lady Giselle, I know you must be wondering why I came to Bath so precipitously and after so short an acquaintance with Miss Freemantle. As soon as I set eyes on her I knew she was the one for me. It was a *coup de foudre* – there is nothing either of us can do about it. We are destined to be together and I intend to marry your cousin before I leave for the continent, and then she may accompany me.'

She was so startled by this extraordinary announcement she stopped, causing the young lady promenading behind her to tread on the back of her skirt and there was an ominous tearing sound. After apologies on both sides, Giselle retreated in the hope that Jenny could repair the damage.

In the chaos that had followed the collision she had not had the opportunity to express her horror at Lieutenant Sullivan's announcement. She grabbed Beth's elbow.

'Please come with me. I need your help to mend my gown.

See – it is horribly torn and we might have to return if it cannot be repaired.'

Her cousin could hardly struggle in so public a place, so reluctantly accompanied Giselle to the ladies' retiring room. Once there she dragged her cousin into an alcove where they could not be overheard.

'I've just heard the most arrant nonsense from that young gentleman. The duke will be here tomorrow morning and he will put a stop to any thoughts of eloping.'

'How could you do that? I thought you were my friend. I will never forgive you for ruining my happiness like this.'

She tried to pull her arm away but Giselle hung on tightly. Anna, Beth's maid, and Jenny appeared and together they bundled the protesting girl from the premises. Carstairs must have seen Giselle all but drag Beth from the dance floor and was waiting in the vestibule.

'Mr Carstairs, Miss Freemantle has decided that she wishes to elope with the cavalry officer she met on the journey down. We must return at once to the house.'

He stepped in and took Beth's arm and pulled it through his own. 'You will come with me, Miss Freemantle, quietly, and we will make our way back to our house. I am sure on reflection you will understand we have prevented you from making a disastrous mistake.'

With Giselle on her other side, the footman in front, and the two maids close behind, her cousin had little option but to do as she was bid. As soon as they were inside she snatched her arm away, picked up her skirts and raced upstairs sobbing wildly.

'Anna, go with your mistress and make sure she remains in her bedchamber. Do you understand?' The girl curtsied and ran off without comment. 'Jenny, I shall be up directly. Please wait for me upstairs.' Her maid also hurried away.

'This whole thing is like something out of a romantic novel, Mr Carstairs. Two sensible people could not possibly decide to spend the rest of their lives together after an acquaintance of a few hours. We know nothing about the young man apart from what he has told us – do you think he is a fortune hunter?'

'I have no idea, my lady, but you nipped this in the bud and I believe Miss Freemantle and the family will come out of it unscathed. However, I think it would be wise to send for the duke.'

'He is on his way and should be here sometime tomorrow. Thank you for your timely assistance. I shall retire and we will reconvene in the morning. I think I might lock Miss Freemantle's door tonight just to be sure she will not creep away.'

There was no key on the outside of the door and when she tried to open it, it would not budge. Beth must have jammed a chair under the door handle to prevent her entering. She was too restless to sleep and so changed into a morning gown and decided to go down to the library and find herself something to read. There was bound to be something on the flora and fauna of the area that would be of interest.

Sometime later she was about to leave the library when she heard a strange thumping noise outside the windows. She quickly extinguished her candle and went to investigate. There was sufficient moonlight to show her what was happening out there – there was a ladder being positioned against the wall. There were not one, but two gentlemen outside.

Her mouth was dry and her palms damp. The wretched lieutenant had brought along a friend to help him abscond with Beth. Once her cousin was in the carriage it would be too late.

She ran to the servants' stairs and raced up them, glad there was still the occasional wall sconce alight. When she entered her cousin's bedchamber via the dressing room she saw that

Beth was on her bed asleep, but she was fully dressed and there was a valise by the window. As soon as the knock came her cousin would depart, unless she could fetch someone to help her prevent it.

There was no time to do that. If she was to prevent this disastrous elopement she must do something herself. Beth's evening cloak had been abandoned on the carpet. She snatched it up and swirled it around her shoulders then hastily pulled up the hood. With the overnight bag in one hand she stepped out onto the small balcony, pulling the window closed behind her.

* * *

London

Rushton set out for Grosvenor Square with Silchester three days after the girls had departed for Bath. He was looking forward to spending a week or so in Town, visiting his clubs and catching up with the gossip. They clattered into the stable yard at midday. He dismounted and tossed his reins to a waiting groom.

'Have you plans for this afternoon, Silchester?'

'I have nothing arranged for today, but I do have several business meetings tomorrow. I thought that we might stroll around to St James's Street and visit our clubs.'

'Excellent notion – it is too long since I visited either Boodle's or White's. The Season is drawing to a close, so I expect that many of our acquaintances will have already departed for their country estates.'

'The House is still sitting and until it recesses most of our cronies will remain. How long is it since you attended?'

'Too long. And you?'

'I go when asked. The prime minister is aware that I am available if necessary.'

An hour later his valet, Penrose, had worked his usual magic and Rushton was once more immaculate.

'I know it is *de rigueur* for one to carry a cane and top hat, Penrose, but I cannot be bothered with such niceties. I shall do very well as I am.'

He was not given to sartorial splendour, but, like most of his peers, had his clothes tailored at Weston's and his boots made by Hoby. As this shop was also in the same street, he thought he might call in and order another pair of riding boots.

His lips curved when he saw Silchester waiting in the vast entrance hall for his arrival. Not only were they of similar age, build and height, they were dressed identically. Both in dark blue topcoats, grey silk waistcoats and a froth of snowy white neckcloth.

'I apologise if I kept you waiting, my friend. I am sharp-set – do we eat at White's? They do a fine beef pie that I'm rather partial to.'

After a brisk walk, they arrived at their destination. The club was surprisingly busy. The appetising aroma of beef pie wafted from the dining room, and from the volume of noise, the place was already busy.

Luncheon was as good as he'd hoped but he found the noise and smoke-filled rooms unpleasant. He told Silchester he was going to order his boots and left him in a lively discussion about the war on the Peninsula. It must be a concern for the family having one of the twins roaming around spying on the French. If Lord Perry was apprehended by the enemy, he would be shot. Although, of course, if he was fighting on the front line he was just as likely to be killed or wounded anyway.

He was emerging from Hoby's when someone called his

name. He looked round in surprise to see a smartly dressed lady of middle years, completely unknown to him, hurrying in his direction.

'I beg your pardon for accosting you so rudely, Lord Rushton, but I must speak to you. I should really speak to the Duke of Silchester but cannot bring myself to do so.'

He drew her to one side so they were not obliging other pedestrians to walk around them. 'We are not acquainted, I believe. Therefore, you have the advantage of me.'

'I am Lady Augusta, I'm married to Colonel Sullivan. My son is a lieutenant in the cavalry and he is planning to elope with Miss Freemantle. I know nothing about this young lady, but to do something so beyond the pale will surely ruin his career and her reputation.'

'You did right to come to me, my lady. However, I'm at a loss to know how your son and Miss Freemantle can have developed so close an association in so short a time.'

'It would seem that they met by chance and, according to his letter, he fell instantly in love with her and followed her to Bath.'

'I see. I shall inform the duke and then we will travel to Bath and prevent this disaster.' He nodded, she curtsied and he strode back into the club.

He was greeted by the doorman who handed him a note. It was from Silchester telling him he had been called away to Parliament and would be unavailable for the next three days. This was an unmitigated disaster. There was no option but for him to step in and resolve this nonsense himself. He could hardly drag Silchester out from an emergency meeting with the government.

On his return to Grosvenor Square he set things in motion. Going by horseback would be faster even if this would mean exchanging his mount more than once on the journey. Penrose must follow with his baggage in the carriage.

After quickly scribbling an explanation for Silchester he was ready to depart. If he rode through the night he should be there at dawn. He prayed that he would be in time to stop Miss Freemantle. Did Giselle know what her cousin was planning? Surely not – she was a sensible young lady and would not countenance such an outlandish scheme.

* * *

Bath

When he clattered into the stable yard in Queen Square he was obliged to shout for attention. He had heard a church clock strike six a short time ago and was confident he had made the best time he possibly could.

He swung to the ground and his knees all but buckled beneath him. He swore under his breath. 'Take care of this horse. He has served me well.'

'Yes, sir. Was we expecting you?' The groom scratched his head. 'No one told me we was having a visitor so early.'

'It's none of your damn business. Get on with your work and mind your tongue.' The man jumped as if poked by a sharp stick and pulled his forelock.

'Begging your pardon, your honour. I'll see to your horse meself.' The groom snapped his fingers and the stable boy appeared rubbing his eyes. 'Take the gentleman to the house. You'll need to bang on the kitchen door, I reckon.'

Rushton supposed he should have waited for a servant to open the side door but he had been travelling too long and was too tired to bother about etiquette. He strode through the kitchen giving the cook and her scullery maids barely a glance and emerged in the entrance hall.

He could hardly bang on the bedchamber doors, but he needed to know if he was in time.

* * *

London

Beau returned to Grosvenor Square in the small hours two days after he had abandoned his friend in St James's Street. The house was locked but he made his way to the side door and knocked loudly. There was always a footman sleeping in an armchair close by for this eventuality.

The unfortunate young man who had been given this duty greeted him with unexpected enthusiasm.

'Good morning, your grace. This letter came by express. It arrived a few hours ago.'

Beau nodded his thanks and took the letter from the silver salver the footman was holding out. The sconces were burning in this part of the house, so he snapped open the seal and read the contents.

Beau,

I am writing to ask if you could come at once to Bath. I fear that Beth has deceived us all about her true character and she is indeed the flighty young lady we once thought her to be.

She will not behave for me but requires your presence to curb her misbehaviour. I look forward with eager anticipation to your arrival.

Your loving sister,

Giselle

God's teeth! What was the wretched girl doing that had so alarmed his normally composed sister that she had written such a letter? He took the back stairs and hammered on the door of his friend's bedchamber. When he received no response, he flung it open.

The room was empty; the bed had not been slept in. Where the devil was Rushton? He had no option but to set out for Somerset in answer to this plea. It would be dawn in a couple of hours so there was little point in retiring – he would rouse his valet and get him to pack his trunk. Hopefully his man would know what had happened to Rushton.

Green answered his summons with alacrity. He appeared equally delighted to see his master home. 'Thank the good Lord you are here, your grace. Lord Rushton has left you a note. He has ridden post-haste to Bath.'

He read this second missive and his heart sank. Devil take it! Things were far worse than he had thought. Thank God Rushton had been able to leave ahead of him.

'I shall be going to Bath at first light. Did Lord Rushton's valet take the carriage?'

'He did, your grace. I could travel by post with your luggage.'

'No, he and I are of similar size; I shall borrow from him. I can also share the services of his valet. I suggest that you return to Silchester as that's where I shall need you when this is sorted. Inform the staff that Lady Giselle and Miss Freemantle will also be returning shortly.'

Whilst his man packed the two pouches of a saddlebag with his necessities, he changed his garments. He had not eaten for several hours so devoured some cold cuts and bread before heading for the stables. He was not travelling alone; this would be unwise for someone in his position, so a groom was waiting for him.

Together they clattered through the archway onto the road and began the long journey to Bath. When he stopped to exchange his mount for a fresh one he was delighted to find that Rushton's horse was there. He took this – no one argued about his right to do so – and embarked on the second stage of his long ride.

He bitterly regretted his impulsive decision to allow his sister and his cousin to go away without him to supervise their activities. What had possessed him to add Rushton's daughters to the mix? He was the man of sense, famous for his diplomacy, and yet he had made the most foolish of choices and now his family was embroiled in a scandal of monumental proportions.

6

BATH

Rushton had no choice. If he selected the incorrect door so be it. There were three doors and as he hesitated the one furthest away was flung open and Miss Freemantle burst out, her face tear-streaked, her expression anguished. His mad race through the darkness had not been in vain. The first thing he noticed was that she was dressed in a travelling ensemble and had her bonnet on.

'Lord Rushton, the most dreadful thing has happened. Lady Giselle has run away with my future husband. How could she do such a thing to me?'

'What the devil do you mean? Stop snivelling, child, and explain yourself.'

His sharp tone was enough to get the girl to stop crying. 'I had arranged to elope with my beloved tonight but she went in my place. Come, you can see the ladder outside my bedroom and my bag has gone too.'

He pushed past and went to the open window. Sure enough, there was a ladder propped against the balcony. 'Have you checked her room?'

The girl looked at him as if he were a simpleton. 'Lord Rushton, my bag did not vanish of its own volition. There's no need to check Giselle's bedchamber – she has gone. I am certain of it.'

He grabbed her by the arm and pushed her towards the adjoining door. 'Is this her chamber?' She nodded. 'Then go in and check. I have no wish to set out to search for her if she is in fact still here and had merely removed your baggage to prevent you leaving.'

His words made sense to her and she pushed open the door. Up until that moment he had hoped Miss Freemantle was mistaken and that Giselle was safely in her bed. The chamber was empty – the bed had not been disturbed.

He turned the air blue and made no apology for it. 'Tell me where you were intending to go with Sullivan. Now – do not procrastinate.'

'We were going to his country estate in Kent. Once we had spent the night together unchaperoned the duke and his parents would have had no recourse but to allow us to be married. There was no need to travel all the way to Scotland.'

'Where in Kent exactly?'

'I believe he said he lived close to the village called Ashburton and his estate is Ashburton Manor.'

If he set out immediately on horseback he might well overtake them before they reached their destination. A plain woman in her bedrobe appeared at his side.

'Forgive me for intruding, sir. I am Miss Gibbons, governess to Lord Rushton's daughters. Can I be of any assistance?'

'Take care of Miss Freemantle, if you would. Get her into her bedchamber and make sure she stays there.'

As he reached the entrance hall, Carstairs appeared more or less correctly dressed. Rushton quickly explained what had transpired.

'My horse is up to your weight, my lord. Take him. If you cut across country, you should catch them before they reach Reading. They will have to stop more than once to change horses and will be obliged to stay overnight at least twice. It is nigh on two hundred miles – a goodly distance to travel. I'm sure you will be in time to prevent a disaster.'

'My man should arrive with the carriage at some point. Have him come after me with Lady Giselle's maid and her trunk. The duke will also be arriving and will wish to follow.'

He was bone-weary after riding over one hundred miles and had not slept for two days. Much as he would like to, if he attempted to leave without resting for a while he could fall from his horse and break his neck, which would help no one.

Carstairs was horrified to think he had made the journey from London without respite. 'The housekeeper has all the guest rooms prepared, my lord. She will take you to one and you must sleep. They can have only been gone an hour...'

Rushton punched the wall. The pain was enough to dispel his fatigue. 'We have got this wrong. Of course Lady Giselle has not run away, she substituted herself for Miss Freemantle in order to prevent her cousin from leaving. The deception will have been discovered by now and the gentleman in question will hardly continue on his journey with the wrong young lady in his possession.'

'You are right, sir. You could very well meet them on their return if you set out immediately.'

The house was now ablaze with candlelight and both the housekeeper and butler were standing about agog for information. The staff were unknown to any of them – they did not owe loyalty to the family. Word of Giselle's exploits would be all over Bath by tonight if he did not do something immediately to prevent it.

He came to a decision. He nodded to Carstairs. 'Get that ladder moved to the window of the guest room I shall be using. Do it yourself.' The man slipped away, understanding immediately why he had made this strange request.

Rushton turned to the housekeeper and butler. 'I apologise for rousing the household in this way. I am here to see my daughters. I miss them dreadfully and could not stay away another minute and wish to be here when they get up. Please conduct me to a chamber and the rest of you must return to your beds immediately.'

Ten minutes later he had climbed out of the window and made his way down the path that led around the house and into the square upon which all the houses faced. The sun was about to rise and soon there would be servants and other tradespeople abroad. If Lady Giselle was seen her reputation would be gone.

His intention was to escort her down the path and up the ladder so she could be safely in her bedchamber before her maid came in with her morning chocolate. He prayed his assessment of the situation was correct and that Lieutenant Sullivan was not a villain, but a young man foolishly in love.

His assumptions were correct as he had not been lurking in the shrubbery for more than a quarter of an hour when a carriage lurched into the square. The team were lathered; they had been driven hard. The vehicle rocked to a halt some distance from the house, the carriage door was opened from the inside and Giselle was all but thrown out.

He was at her side and had his arm around her waist to support her before the carriage was in motion. 'Quickly, sweetheart, we must get you inside. You will have to ascend the ladder, but if luck is on our side, you will come out of this unscathed.'

'Lord Rushton, how are you here? I sent for my brother.'

'I shall explain it all to you once you are safely indoors.'

Then disaster struck. As they were walking briskly past the neighbour's house the front door opened and a gentleman stepped out. It was too late to hide. Giselle's hood had fallen back and he knew at once she had been recognised.

He nodded politely as if unbothered by being seen at dawn returning to the house with an unmarried young lady on his arm. 'We must brazen this out, Giselle.' She was rigid beneath his touch but nodded.

'I hope the duke does not call me out for making you an offer before he has given his permission, my love.'

Her eyes widened but she gallantly followed his lead. 'I think my brother will be surprised that we have such strong feelings for each other, but he will be happy for us.'

She had spoken loudly enough to be overheard by the watcher. He sincerely hoped this would be enough to explain them being outside at this time. He guided her through the front gate and up the path – there was little point in using the ladder now they had been seen.

Carstairs must have been watching and the door was opened as they approached. Although only Silchester's man was waiting to greet them in the hall, he was aware they were being observed from the shadows.

'You must be the first to congratulate us, Carstairs. Lady Giselle has done me the honour of accepting my offer. My decision to escort Lady Giselle for an early morning walk gave us an ideal opportunity to speak of our feelings.'

'Congratulations, my lord, my lady. The duke will be delighted to hear the news when he arrives later today.'

As Rushton gently released his future wife she stared up at him. Her eyes were tear-filled. She was as wretched about this as he was, but they had no choice. She managed a watery smile and ran lightly up the stairs. He followed more slowly, desperate to find his bed and catch a few hours' sleep before facing the wrath of his friend.

Only as he closed his eyes did he recall that his sudden appearance at the front door, when he had only recently been escorted into his bedchamber upstairs, would be puzzling the watchers. The fact that Giselle had also magically appeared at his side was a conundrum he hoped they would not solve.

* * *

Jenny was waiting for Giselle when she entered her bedchamber. 'I expect you would like to bathe, my lady, and then retire. You must be quite exhausted after your exciting...'

'I shall bathe, but you would do well to remember your place if you wish to retain it.' She fixed the girl with a frosty stare and was understood instantly. Giselle was indeed exhausted, but far worse than that was the fact that her life was in tatters. Her foolishness had pushed poor Lord Rushton into an untenable position. He'd had no option but to make her an offer or both their reputations would have been gone.

She prayed that when her brother arrived he could find a way out of this disaster. Lord Rushton was a handsome man, wealthy and would make someone an ideal husband – but not her. In her imagination she had thought herself attracted to him but in the reality of the situation she realised she considered him as no more than a friend of the family.

Having a bath was a luxury and she knew she should have remained in it for more than a few minutes, but she wished to get into the privacy of her bed and draw the curtains around her. Knowing her cousin as she did, Beth would want to come and speak to her soon as she was up, and the last thing she wished was to see was the perpetrator of this catastrophe.

No doubt Lord Rushton would retire as well. She sat up, sending a cascade of water over the floor, as something occurred to her. How had he come to be outside her house at dawn? She changed her mind about going to bed.

'Jenny, I wish to speak to Lord Rushton immediately.' Her maid's eyes widened in shock. 'I shall get dressed, but my nightgown and bedrobe will suffice. Lord Rushton and I are betrothed so there can be no objection to him coming to my sitting room.'

There was barely time for her to reach this chamber before there was a loud knock on the door. 'Come in, my lord, I must speak to you on a matter of the utmost urgency.'

He strode in. He too had obviously been in the process of disrobing, for he had no stock around his neck and no waistcoat either. 'What is it? I should not be in here especially as you are improperly dressed.'

'Please, sit down, sir. We have much to talk about before Beau arrives. I wish to know how you came to be here this morning and no doubt you would like to know how I came to be in this predicament.'

The news that Lieutenant Sullivan had informed his mother of his plans before he had even reached Bath was quite astonishing. 'I think the young man to be touched in the attic. There can be no other explanation for his extraordinary behaviour. Although, I own that he does appear to be genuinely in love with my cousin.'

He was unsurprised by how she had come to be in the carriage but was interested to hear Sullivan's reaction when he discovered the deception.

'I was able to keep my hood over my face for some distance. I deliberately sat on the far side of the carriage and he made no attempt to embrace me. We sat in silence for half an hour and then I decided to reveal my identity. To say that he was horrified is an understatement.'

'I'm surprised that he did not insist that he had compromised you beyond redemption and would marry you instead of Miss Freemantle.'

'He did indeed suggest that, reluctantly, but with all sincerity. I told him I had no wish to marry him and that he should return me at once. He banged on the roof of the carriage and when it stopped he got out and I didn't see him again. I've no idea whether he travelled on the box, or strode off into the darkness by himself.'

'I was once in love myself, my dear, but it is not something I wish to experience again. It is better left to those young enough to endure the pain when it ends.'

'I am not given to such flights of fancy either, sir, and we must be pragmatic about what has happened. Your girls deserve to have a mama who will love them and I am prepared to take on that role. I shall be one and twenty on my next birthday and it is high time that I had my own establishment. Therefore, I accept your kind offer, but wish to make it clear it will be a marriage in name only.' She swallowed a lump in her throat and forced herself to continue. 'I shall be forever grateful that you stepped in and saved my good name and that the family will not be brought into disrepute. You're making the ultimate sacrifice on my behalf.'

For the first time he smiled and looked less forbidding. 'Do you wish me to get down on one knee?'

'No, my lord, I'm content with how things stand. I will do my best to be a good wife to you...' His eyes flashed and he raised an eyebrow. 'Apart from sharing your bed, that is. I might be an innocent, but I know that a gentleman can satisfy those needs elsewhere.'

'Good God! This is a highly unsuitable topic of conversation; I am not sure if I am shocked or impressed by your sophistication.'

'I believe that we must have everything clear between us before the duke arrives.'

He nodded and yawned and covered his mouth. 'I will be honest with you, Giselle, I'm not an easy man to live with. I'm given to dark moods and prefer to be solitary. However, I will not stand in your way if you wish to entertain and will take a house in Town for next Season if you wish me to.'

'Then everything is settled between us. There is something I think we must discuss – indeed, it is the reason that I called you here. As far as the staff were concerned they believed that I was sleeping in bed and that you had retired. How are we to explain our presence outside? We can hardly mention we both exited via a ladder.'

'I think we brazen it out, sweetheart. As long as Miss Freemantle's name is not mentioned, and we are officially betrothed, then the whys and wherefores are nobody's business but ours.'

She tried to hide her own yawn and failed miserably. He stood up and pointed towards her bedchamber. 'Go to bed. You will need your wits about you when your brother arrives. God help Miss Freemantle when he discovers why we are so precipitously engaged.' She wanted to ask him when they were to be wed but he shook his head.

'Away with you, little one, we are both too fatigued to talk sensibly any longer. We will reconvene at midday.' He nodded, raised his hand in farewell and strolled out as if his life was not destroyed. Perhaps if he could accept what had happened with equanimity and good humour she could do the same.

* * *

Surprisingly, she slept soundly and did not wake until Beth burst in wailing and crying. Giselle pushed herself onto her elbows and fixed her cousin with a steely glance.

'Stop that at once, Elizabeth. It is not you who is now obliged to marry a man you do not love and who does not love you. Your stupidity has put Rushton and myself in this invidious position; you should be on your knees begging my forgiveness and not wailing at how *I* have ruined *your* life.'

'You don't understand. The duke is here, and he is terrifying in his fury. I am to be sent to a seminary as soon as we get back to Silchester Court. He will not even allow me to return to my mama's estate.' Beth collapsed in an undignified heap on the carpet. 'I know you don't understand such things, but Theodore and I are irrevocably in love. He will go to war and I might never see him again. I shall not recover from this and will never forgive you for preventing me...'

'Silence. Remove yourself and return to your room until you are told you can leave it.' Beau's voice cracked like a whip and Beth flinched. Without another word she scrambled to her feet and ran from the bedchamber.

Giselle swallowed a sob. Then he was beside her on the bed and his arms were around her, giving her the comfort she so desperately needed.

'I am so sorry this has happened to you, but you must be brave. Rushton is a good man and I would not give my permission if I thought he wouldn't make you a good husband.'

She gulped and rubbed her wet cheeks on his shoulder. 'I don't want to marry him; I don't want to marry anyone. He doesn't want to marry me either. We shall both be miserable. It would have been better to have let Beth run away...'

'Perhaps it would have been, but you could not let her do it any more than Rushton could stand aside when you were in trouble. A lot of marriages start with respect and friendship and real affection comes after time. This is not what I wanted for you – he is too old for you – but he will take good care of you if you let him. I believe he could make you happy.'

7

After an uncomfortable interview with Silchester, Rushton went in search of his daughters. They must hear from himself that they were about to get a new mama. The governess curtsied and made herself scarce, leaving him alone with the girls in the schoolroom.

Before he could greet them, they dropped their slates and were across the room and into his arms.

'Papa, we didn't know you were coming. We are so glad to see you,' Estelle said. 'We hope you haven't come to take us home just yet, as we are having the best time. We love Miss Gibbons and want to bring her back with us.'

'I missed you both and am delighted to find you are having such a good time.' He picked them up, not an easy feat as they were becoming heavier by the month, and carried them to the wooden settle under the windows. With one on either side of him he was ready to tell them the news.

'My loves, I have the most exciting news for you. Lady Giselle and I are to be married – she is to be your new mama.'

There was no hesitation from either of them. Their squeals

of delight and the kisses they smothered him with told him all he wanted to know. Whatever his feelings about this match, his children would be happy.

'When are you getting married, Papa?' Eloise asked.

'I'm not sure, but as soon as we return to Silchester Court, I should think. The duke is considering the options as it is his prerogative to dictate how events unfold. Lady Giselle has not quite reached her majority so must have his permission to be wed.'

'Can we be flower girls, Papa? Will there be a big party afterwards? Can we come with you on your wedding trip?'

'Enough questions, Estelle. I shall give you the answers when I know them myself. But I can tell you most assuredly that you will not be accompanying us on our wedding trip, if we take one.'

The governess was waiting to speak to him outside in the passageway. 'Excuse me, my lord, but I am well aware my appointment is just for the summer. I promise I did not set the children up to ask you…'

'Miss Gibbons, I was about to go down on bended knee to beg you to come back to Castlemere. The girls are happier than they have ever been in anyone else's charge. Lady Giselle will speak to you about our plans when they are clearer.'

'Thank you, my lord, it will be my pleasure to continue to educate your delightful daughters. Although I have only known them a few days, already I am well aware how bright they both are.'

Rushton left the nursery floor satisfied that the most important people in his life would benefit from this arrangement. It was a wretched business indeed for both Giselle and himself to be forced into a union they did not really want. She was undoubtedly a beautiful young lady, intelligent, kind – in fact everything one could want in a bride. If she was but five years older he would be less concerned. She was far too young for him; he had watched her grow up and would always see her as a girl from a different generation to him, more like a niece than a wife.

Her sister and two brothers had married in the past two years and all were love matches. He was sure she had hoped to do the same and now she was saddled with him. He was the fortunate one – it was she who would miss out on all the things a young lady dreamed off. Her romantic dreams were in tatters and there was little he could do about it. He would treat her with loving kindness, allow her the freedom to do as she pleased within reason, but he had no intention of consummating the union. It would be like making love to a girl, not a woman grown.

It was past noon and he was sharp-set. He had still been abed when breakfast had been served and he sincerely hoped there would be some sort of luncheon provided. Silchester had said Miss Freemantle, the cause of all this chaos, was to be sent to a seminary to mend her ways. In some households she would have been beaten by her guardian, so she was fortunate the duke had not done so as she richly deserved to be punished. Her wild behaviour had ruined the lives of himself and Giselle, and that was something the family would never forgive.

Carstairs was hovering in the entrance hall. 'Lord Rushton, could you spare me a moment of your time? Perhaps we could go to the study where we can talk in privacy.'

'Lead the way. There are things I wish to discuss with you too.'

Silchester's man of business would know what his master planned and would no doubt already have a date in mind for the nuptials.

* * *

Giselle was somewhat comforted by her brother's words but nothing he said would stop the feeling of utter despair when she thought of what was facing her in the near future. He was right, Lord Rushton would make her an excellent husband, and no doubt there were dozens of young ladies around the country who would swap with her in a second.

If she had considered the kind of man she would one day marry it would not have been someone thirteen years her senior, a widower with two half-grown children who was still in love with his long-departed wife. She blinked back unwanted tears. Her siblings had married because they were in love with their future partners and she had secretly wished to do the same.

How was it possible that a week ago she had thought of him so fondly, yet now she was obliged to marry him he no longer seemed so appealing?

Too late to repine – the matter was settled and she had no option but to marry a friend of her brother's and make the best of it. She had told him she had no wish to share his bed, but at some point in the future this must change as she would like children of her own. He had no direct heir; he must be keen to rectify this matter and was being a true gentleman by agreeing to her request.

Jenny fussed over her appearance but it hardly mattered – it wasn't as if she wished to impress anyone. Rushton would have to marry her even if she dressed as Miss Gibbons had when she arrived. What had the children thought of the announcement? Really, she should go up and speak to them, but she didn't have the energy to do so just now.

As she passed the door of her cousin's bedchamber she

wondered if she should go in and speak to her. Although it was the girl's fault she was in this predicament, if she hadn't interfered and allowed Beth to run away then things would have been so much better for all of them. Beth would be married to the man she loved, and she and Rushton would not be forced into a union where there was love on neither side. There was respect and affection, and she must believe this was enough to make the union bearable.

She tapped on the door and there was the sound of footsteps, and then it was opened by Beth herself. Giselle had expected to see her cousin distraught but instead she was composed.

'I am so glad you have come to see me, dearest Giselle. Will the duke object to you speaking to me? I've no wish to get you into further strife.'

'I should come and see you regardless of his opinion, Beth. Where is your maid? Why didn't she open the door?'

'I have sent her away – I've no wish to have her fluttering around me. Please, would you sit down?'

The way her cousin was speaking was quite out of character but Giselle did as she was bid. 'I came because I have realised that my interference has ruined not just my life and that of Lord Rushton, but also yours and that of Lieutenant Sullivan.'

Beth smiled sadly. 'If I had not been such a wilful, stupid girl none of this would have happened. Theodore and I behaved appallingly, let our feelings overrun our common sense. We should not have even contemplated running away together after so short an acquaintance. If we had behaved as we should, I could have introduced him to the duke and he could have introduced me to his mama – now all is ruined and it is entirely our own fault.'

'And if I had not taken it upon myself to interfere then we

would all have been happy. My brother and his mother would have got used to the idea in time. I have vowed that in future I shall never allow my actions to be dictated to by what society might consider appropriate.' She embraced her cousin and for a few moments they stood with their arms around each other, renewing their relationship.

'You do not deserve to be unhappy, Giselle, but I do. I shall go to the seminary and be as miserable as I can be, as it is my just deserts. I will not hold in my heart the thought that one day Theodore and I will be together as man and wife. No, one day I shall marry because I have to – love will not come into it.'

'Good heavens! There is no necessity to be so melodramatic, my love. I intend to speak to Beau and have him rescind his order that you leave. I shall marry Lord Rushton willingly; I could not ask for a kinder and more suitable husband than him. As you know I have long harboured a secret admiration for him...'

'I didn't know that, but now I come to think of it, dearest, I do recall that in London last year you danced with him on several occasions and appeared to enjoy the experience. Now I do not feel so guilty. However, I think it might be best if I do go away, so could you possibly suggest to the duke that I visit my mama? After all, she lives in this county and it will not take more than a few hours to get there from Bath.'

'An excellent notion. I'm sure your adopted mother will be delighted to see you, especially as Mary is away with Aubrey for the foreseeable future.'

'I've always considered Mary to be my real sister, even though she is not. When you are married, there will only be Lord Aubrey's twin, Lord Peregrine, and the duke himself, left without wives. I do not count of course, as I am a Freemantle and not a Sheldon like the rest of you.'

'You are part of the family even if you have a different name, Beth. Why don't you write to Lady Augusta and apologise? You never know, she might soften in her attitude once she knows that you are a genuine young lady and not a fortune hunter.'

'I have the more substantial fortune, Giselle, and my grandfather was a duke. Theodore's grandfather was merely an earl.'

'In which case, it is he who should write to my brother with an apology. It could do no harm for you to do as I suggest, especially if you wish one day to be reunited with this gentleman.'

She left her cousin searching for a pen and paper, and continued on her way downstairs. As she reached the entrance hall her future husband strode in from the direction of the library. 'At last, my dear, I have been waiting this age to speak to you. We have much to discuss – shall we repair to the library?'

He held out his arm and obediently she placed her hand on it. It was as if she was walking beside her oldest brother; she felt not a flicker of excitement at being in such close contact. Whatever fledgling feelings of attraction there might have been last year these had been firmly squashed by this precipitous betrothal.

The door was closed firmly behind and he gestured that she take the seat at the far end of the room, in front of the window that overlooked the garden. She was tempted to sit where she pleased, but thought it wise not to antagonise him with her improper decision to ignore the strict rules of society in future.

'I have spoken to my daughters and they are delighted at the prospect of having you as their mama. Miss Gibbons is now their permanent governess and will accompany us back to Castlemere when we return after our wedding.'

'Why is your house called so? Does it have crenellations and towers?'

He looked somewhat startled by her question, as well he

might, as she had deliberately ignored his comments about his children, their marriage and the governess.

'It does indeed have both things, and a moat running around it. It was built several hundred years ago, but I can assure you the wing in which we live is of modern construction.'

'I shouldn't object if it was not, sir, as I like ancient buildings.' She smiled politely and folded her hands in her lap, but said no more.

His eyes narrowed and something dangerous flickered in his eyes. Perhaps she should be more cooperative, at least until they were married.

'I take it from your lack of response, my lady, that you are not interested in the welfare of your future daughters and...'

'No, how can you say such a thing? I love the girls and it is the one thing about this business that I do not regret.' In her agitation, she jumped to her feet and began to pace the room.

'Sit down, Giselle, you're making me dizzy. We cannot talk sensibly whilst you are perambulating about the place like this.'

She stopped a few yards from him and fixed him with her fiercest stare. 'I am not a child to be dictated to. I am a woman grown and expect to be treated like one, not like one of your daughters.'

Before she could react, he was on his feet and inches from her. 'Do you indeed?'

His breath was warm on her face; he was too close; he was making her feel hot all over. She had never been so near a gentleman before, apart from one of her brothers. She took an involuntary step away from him but he followed her until she could go no further, as her back was pressed against the wall.

He placed a hand either side of her, trapping her within his arms. Her heart was hammering so hard she could scarcely breathe. She closed her eyes in the vain hope that this would discourage him. His intent was obvious – he intended to kiss her and that was the last thing she wanted.

Her body reacted of its own volition. Her legs crumpled beneath her and she slithered down until she was sitting on the floor.

He reached down and hoisted her up. He was no longer predatory but laughing at her. 'As I thought, my dear, you are no more a woman grown than I am. Now sit down, like a good girl, so we can talk about what is going to happen.'

This time she took a chair as far away from him as was possible and he could barely hide his amusement at her childish gesture. 'Do we really have to get married? Surely if we remain betrothed for a month or two I can then jilt you and both our reputations will remain intact?'

His expression was sympathetic, but he shook his head. 'Believe me, sweetheart, if it were possible to do as you suggest it would be done. Unfortunately, word has already spread around the square about us being abroad at dawn unchaperoned. There is no other way out of this for either of us.'

'I do not see why we should be forced into a union neither of us want just to conform to what society considers proper. I am the daughter of a duke; you are a peer of the realm. I cannot believe that whatever we do we will not be accepted by our friends and neighbours. I don't care if my reputation is temporarily ruined as I have no intention of looking for a husband. When I do meet the gentleman I shall fall in love with, he will love me regardless of any scandal.'

'That's as may be, but I have no wish to be considered a debaucher of young women. I have my daughters to consider and have no intention of besmirching their name. You must also remember your family – it would not only be you who was tainted, but everyone associated with you.'

'That is nonsense, sir. My family can send me away to one of our estates in the north and the matter will be settled. I rather think that this episode will make you more attractive to the young ladies of the *ton*. I've often heard it said that there is nothing admired more than a rake – especially one who is rich, titled, eligible and handsome.' She stood and faced him squarely. 'I have decided I do not care what the consequences are – I shall not marry you.'

8

Giselle stalked to the door but he was there before her, his bulk blocking her passage. She refused to be cowed by his proximity. She raised her head and stared directly at him. 'Kindly remove yourself, sir. This is not the behaviour of a gentleman.'

He remained where he was, relaxed and with a smile in his eyes. He was not angry, merely amused at her antics as if she was one of his daughters playing pranks. She took a steadying breath whilst deciding what action to take next.

She shrugged and turned her back on him, and with every appearance of nonchalance strolled to the bell strap. She tugged it before he realised what she was about. He would have to move when someone came in answer to her summons.

The knock came sooner than she expected. Someone had been lurking outside the door eavesdropping on their conversation. She smiled sweetly at him and he stepped aside. She could not tell from his expression what he was feeling, but she suspected he was not pleased at her stratagem.

The footman held the door open and she sailed through, confident she had extricated herself from an unwanted marriage. They would have to remain engaged for a few weeks but then she would be free.

All that remained was speak to Beau. Lord Rushton could remain with them in Bath, escort her around the place a bit, and when this farce was over he could take his daughters and return to his estate in Essex.

Her brother was in the drawing room and beckoned her. 'You look happier than you did this morning, sweetheart. Have you changed your mind about this marriage?'

'Not at all. I have decided I shall not wed him whatever the consequences. Why should the dictates of society force us to marry when there is no love on either side? We both deserve better than that.'

She braced herself for his anger, his arguments, but instead he took her hands in his and shook his head. 'I wish it was so simple, little sister. I have no wish to make you do something that is abhorrent to you, but I don't think you have considered what your decision would do to this family and to Rushton's.'

'I have suggested to him that we remain betrothed for a few weeks and then I will jilt him. That way he will be the innocent party and I can remove myself to one of our estates in the north until the dust settles.'

'Devil take it! That might just work – I take it Rushton is in agreement?'

'I am not, Silchester.' Rushton had joined them and neither of them had noticed his arrival. 'We were observed returning from an assignation together at dawn.' He glanced at her. 'Forgive me for speaking plainly, my dear, but I can think of no other way to make you understand.

'The assumption will be that we have pre-empted the marriage bed – for what other reason would we have left the house in the middle of the night together?'

This was the outside of enough. She snatched her hands away from Beau's and scrambled to her feet. 'Why should we choose to leave the comfort of this house, which has a dozen empty bedchambers, if that was our intention?'

Her brother was now on his feet and standing protectively beside her. 'That is a valid point, Rushton. Come, my friend, we have found a way out of this situation; why are you not taking it eagerly? It is my sister who will suffer the temporary loss of her good name – you will come out of it unscathed.'

'Lord Rushton, there's no need for you to sacrifice your happiness on my account. I appreciate your gallantry – we both do – but the matter is settled. We will parade around Bath to settle the gossips and then we will go our separate ways. In the autumn we will let it be known our betrothal is cancelled.'

'I can see I am outnumbered. There is one thing neither of you have considered in this deceit. My girls are overjoyed at the thought of having you for their mama. They will be devastated when you disappear from their lives.'

He was correct; she had not considered how this arrangement would affect the girls. 'I'm sorry for that, sir, but I sincerely believe it will be better for them to be unhappy for a short while than for us to be unhappy for a lifetime.'

Her throat was choked. She couldn't continue this conversation without showing her distress. She fled, leaving her brother and Rushton together. One thing was certain: this debacle would have irretrievably damaged their friendship and for this she was sorry. The blame was hers; she should have left well alone.

She was halfway up the stairs when the two girls and Miss Gibbons appeared in the gallery. The children raced towards her and threw their arms around her waist.

'May we call you mama? We are so excited, aren't we, Eloise? When are you and Papa to be married?'

'Not for a few months, my loves, so you must continue to call me Aunt Giselle for the moment. I have not forgotten I promised we should drive in an open carriage to Bristol this afternoon. If you will give me a few minutes I shall be ready.'

Beth would have to be told, but she was already tardy and didn't wish to keep Miss Gibbons and the girls waiting. When she returned from the excursion would be time enough to explain what had been decided.

* * *

Rushton heard his daughters go past with their governess but couldn't bring himself to face them. He was not a dissembler by nature and the thought of what he was about to do was against everything he believed. A gentleman did not deceive his family and he would rather marry a reluctant bride than be forced into such a position.

'Silchester, I thought better of you. You have put me in an untenable position. I have no option but to go along with this reprehensible scheme your sister has come up with. When it is done, then our friendship will be at an end.'

This man had been as close to him as a brother since they had met when they were up at Oxford years ago. To sever the connection with the Silchester family was going to be hard, but he had no choice. His honour was being impugned by what they were forcing him to do, and this was unacceptable. He would do as they wanted but he wasn't happy about it.

He retired to his chamber, too dispirited to leave the house and enjoy the warm April sunshine. He was awoken by a frantic banging on his door. What now? Where the hell was his man and why didn't he answer the door as he should?

'Come in.' He was on his feet when the door opened.

A maid he didn't recognise stepped nervously into the room. 'I beg your pardon, my lord, for disturbing you, but I can't find anyone else. His grace has gone out with Mr Carstairs and Lady Giselle and the governess are out with your daughters for the afternoon.'

'What do you want? Why have you disturbed me here?' She wrung her hands and curtsied and he regretted his sharp remark. 'Tell me, what is wrong?'

She responded to his gentler tone. 'It's Miss Freemantle. She has left. I'm Jenny, maid to Lady Giselle. I went to speak to Anna, who looks after Miss Freemantle, and I found the chamber empty. The closets have been cleared, the trunks gone.'

'If she has taken her maid, then there's nothing to worry about. Leave it with me; I'll find out what has transpired.'

He checked the wretched girl's apartment and it was empty. He had expected to find a letter placed conspicuously on the bed, but there was nothing. He would have better luck in the stables as she must have taken a carriage – she could hardly have travelled by public stage with her trunks.

His enquiries revealed that Miss Freemantle had indeed purloined the travelling carriage – she had also taken the coachman, his assistant and the two outriders who had accompanied the Silchester vehicle on its journey here.

The girl had not run away but was going to visit someone, but he was damned if he knew who that might be. Then he recalled she had originally come from this county, that her mother had an estate here. She must have returned to her familial home, which was the first sensible thing she had done in the last twenty-four hours.

Silchester had said he was sending her to a seminary for young ladies, so he didn't blame the girl for departing in this way. He was merely making assumptions, as there appeared to be no letters left for Silchester or his sister. He would wait until one of them returned and let them decide how to deal with the matter.

The day was clement; he could not remain cooped up inside. He would ride out and investigate the countryside, but there was nothing up to his weight in the stables. A groom had already departed with the post horse and eventually would arrive at the inn where he had left his stallion and make the exchange. Obviously, he would be obliged to wait several days before his mount would be sufficiently recovered for him to ride.

The thought of taking a stroll through the city did not appeal and the garden at the rear of the building was too small for his purpose. He would walk, but go in the opposite direction to the Assembly Rooms and hope he met no one who was aware of what had happened that morning.

He was no more than a few yards from the house when he was accosted by a stranger. 'Lord Rushton, might I be the first to congratulate you? We have not been introduced, but I am Sir David Theakston. I reside across the square and heard the good news from his grace when he and his man of business were taking the waters at the Pump Room.' This garrulous gentleman finally paused for breath.

Rushton nodded. 'I thank you for your good wishes, sir. I am a fortunate man indeed to be marrying into one of the most prestigious families in the country.' He nodded again and walked briskly in the opposite direction, having no wish to prolong this conversation.

He remembered his nanny telling him that one falsehood always led to another and that the truth would come out eventually. It had started already. Silchester was making sure any rumours that might have been circulating would be halted by the announcement of his supposed betrothal to Giselle.

There was little he could do about it – the man was taking care of his family and he couldn't fault him for that. After walking rapidly for a mile or two he slowed and began to take in his surroundings. The city of Bath was compact and he was already in the countryside. The sound of the birds singing would normally please him, but he was too angry to take note of them.

Three weeks ago Silchester had come to him with a solution to the problem he was having with his daughters. He had agreed to them going to Bath with only Carstairs to supervise. His daughters were now settled and happy with their new governess and Giselle was right to say they would get over their upset when the engagement was broken.

Could it be that she was also right to demand that he took part in this pretence? His choler slowly dissipated as he considered the facts more rationally. He didn't want a wife, even one as charming as she was, and she certainly didn't want him as a husband.

When he returned he was in a better frame of mind and determined to make a success of this masquerade. He would tender his apologies to Silchester and his sister and hope they would forgive him his curmudgeonly behaviour.

* * *

Giselle had enjoyed the excursion to Bristol, as had Miss Gibbons and the girls, and they all declared it a great success.

'What are we going to do tomorrow, Aunt Giselle?' Estelle asked as the chaise rocked to a standstill outside the house.

'Now, children, do not pester her ladyship. She will wish to spend time with Lord Rushton; as they are so recently betrothed there will be much to discuss about their forthcoming nuptials.'

Fortunately there was no need to answer this comment as, in the flurry of leaving the carriage and walking down the flagged path to the front door, the girls saw their father and rushed to tell him what they had seen and done that afternoon.

Whilst he was engaged with them she was able to slip past unnoticed and was about to scurry upstairs to the sanctuary of her apartment, when her brother waylaid her.

'Beth has gone – do you know where to?'

'She said she was going to return to her mama. I think that a preferable solution to you packing her off to a seminary – she is too old for that now.'

'I wouldn't have done so, sweetheart – you know how I am when I am angry. We need to talk. Shall I accompany you to your apartment?'

'Yes, I would prefer that. Lord Rushton seems happier...'

He shook his head slightly and she took his meaning immediately. Anything that was overheard by the staff, that belonged to this house not to them, would be fodder for the gossip mills of Bath. Once in the safety of her sitting room she continued her comment.

'I'm afraid that we parted on the worst possible terms. I made it clear that I would never marry him under any circumstances.'

Beau chuckled. 'He is like me in that respect, my love; he does not like to be gainsaid. However, he now sees the sense in what you suggested and is prepared to go along with the deception.'

'So, when we return to Silchester it will be over? We will both be free from an unwanted entanglement?'

'We are both hoping so. I don't think you will need to cloister yourself in the north but it would probably be wise to remain at Silchester until the dust settles.'

'I have been thinking about that, Beau, and I would like to travel, not remain at home. Could I not join Aubrey and Mary on their trip around the world?'

'As we have no idea where they are I'm afraid that will be impossible. We have friends in Northumbria, the Darcys, I shall write to them and see if they will extend an invitation. We could also visit the Lakes whilst we are there.'

'Thank you, that is exactly what I should like to do. I am not comfortable here; I believe the servants are spying on us. I wish we had brought our own staff and then none of this would have happened.'

'As you would still have been seen by the neighbour, my dear, that would have made little difference to the outcome. I agree with you; I suggest that we cut short your visit – give the excuse that we need to return to arrange your marriage. We must stay for a week or two and brazen it out.

'Which reminds me, we are attending the ball at the Assembly Rooms this evening. We shall dress to impress and look down our noses at everyone – that should do the trick. It will be remarked that Beth is no longer with us. What are we going to say about that?' Giselle asked.

'I have already dealt with this. I discussed the matter overloudly with Carstairs earlier. I said I had sent her away because of her shocking behaviour.'

'I sincerely hope that they don't ever discover exactly how shocking it would have been. Beth was contrite and I believe her feelings for that young gentleman are sincere. I should have let her go...'

'I agree, I would much prefer my cousin to lose her good

name than my sister. That said, your intervention was courageous and no more than I would expect from you. The next few weeks will be difficult, but not impossible, as you will have me by your side.'

He embraced her briefly and then strode out, leaving her to her thoughts, and they were not happy ones. If there was one thing she hated above all others it was telling falsehoods. Now, not only was she to lie to Estelle and Eloise she must also do the same to everyone she met tonight.

Would she be expected to simper and flutter her eyelids at her future husband? This would be the outside of enough – but if this was supposed to be a love match then they could hardly remain aloof from each other.

There was the sound of the children returning to the nursery floor so their father must be available to speak to. She rang the bell and Jenny appeared from the dressing room. 'Please go downstairs and ask Lord Rushton to attend me here. It is a matter of some urgency.'

The girl curtsied and hurried off to do her bidding. Giselle wasn't quite sure what she would say to this formidable gentleman, but it was imperative they both behaved in the same way. The deception would otherwise be discovered immediately by the eagle-eyed tabbies who sat on the edge of the ballroom floor watching every move of the young ladies and gentlemen dancing upon it.

9

The butler sidled up next to Rushton and spoke quietly into his ear. 'I beg your pardon, my lord, but Lady Giselle would like to speak to you in her apartment at your earliest convenience.'

Rushton nodded, but didn't answer. There was something about this man that he didn't like and he was sure he was behind the eavesdropping and gossip-mongering. He wasn't surprised at this summons as he had intended to seek out Giselle himself before they were obliged to appear in public this evening.

Her sitting room door was ajar. He tapped and pushed it open. She was pacing the carpet as before and his heart went out to her. She was in this invidious position because she had stepped in to save the good name of her cousin. She didn't deserve this – and neither did he.

'Come in, my lord, and thank you for arriving so promptly.'

'I think it is time we refer to each other more informally…'

'I am not going to call you by your given name, if that is what you are suggesting?'

'Nobody calls me Henry. I am known universally as Rushton

and that will do perfectly. I shall address you as Giselle as your family does.'

Her mouth thinned and he thought she was going to protest, but she nodded. 'If we are to dissemble in public this evening we need to decide exactly how to behave. Our sudden engagement could only have taken place for two reasons; one – I have been compromised and left you no alternative but to offer for me. Two – it is a love match and we cannot remain apart a moment longer.'

'I am well aware of that, and obviously, it must be the second version that we use as our script. I suggest...'

'I have no intention of hanging on your arm like a lovesick puppy...'

'Sit down, be quiet and listen for a change.' His abrupt command startled her but she did as he bid without argument. 'Good. I don't know where you got the erroneous impression, my dear, that I would be an accommodating husband. I am master in my own household and would expect a new wife to follow my instructions to the letter.'

She was on her feet again, her eyes flashing. 'As I am not to be your wife, sir, this information is irrelevant. I have decided that I shall treat you as I always do, with respect. That will have to do. I shall dance with you twice, take a turn around the room on your arm, but then I shall claim to have the headache and come home.'

'If you behaved as you are doing now, Giselle, then our subterfuge will have been in vain as it will be clear to all who observe us that we are getting married under duress.'

'Then so be it – I care not for anyone's opinion but my family's.' She nodded towards the door and he had no option but to leave.

He was grinding his teeth in an effort to hold back his fury at her impertinence. How mistaken he was in her character – he had always thought her a well-mannered, sensible young lady but she was proving to be the reverse. The sooner this farce was over the better, and then he could take his girls and return to the sanctuary of his own domain.

At the door, he paused, unable to hide his displeasure. 'Lady Giselle, as far as the world is concerned we are betrothed, which gives me precedence. From now, until our engagement is dissolved, you will answer to me for your behaviour and not your brother.'

For a second she remained still, staring wide-eyed at him. Then she snatched up a large leather-bound book and threw it at his head. He had no opportunity to avoid the missile and it struck him, edge on, full in the face. He lost his balance and fell through the open door to sprawl on his back in the passageway.

The sticky wetness trickling down his face could only be blood. His eyes blurred and it was as if the candles had been doused. The next thing he knew she was on her knees beside him.

'I am so sorry. I don't know why I did that. Here, hold this against the cut whilst I fetch Beau.'

The noise of his fall must surely have been heard elsewhere but for some strange reason no curious servants appeared to investigate. He did as instructed and held the folded towel against his forehead. The next thing he knew the duke was at his side.

'Lie still, my friend. Your valet and mine are here to hoist you to your feet.'

'Forgive me, my lord, but I must put this bandage in place around your head. I fear you will need sutures and a physician has been sent for.'

Penrose, his man, deftly tied the towel in place and then

Rushton was gripped by his elbows and lifted upright. He had expected his head to spin, that he had a concussion, but apart from the wound he believed he was unhurt.

'I am able to walk unaided. I shall return to my apartment and await the ministrations of the doctor when he appears.' The duke looked relieved and well he might.

'Then you will excuse me, Rushton. I need to speak to my sister.'

'No, Silchester, this has nothing to do with you. I will deal with her once the sutures are in place.'

* * *

Giselle heard his words and waited for her brother to contradict Rushton – but he did no such thing.

'You are right. As you are betrothed I shall leave the matter to you.'

The two of them walked down the passageway talking quietly to each other leaving her ashamed and ready to face whatever punishment Rushton thought fit for her crime. Her stomach roiled and for a moment she thought she was about to cast up her accounts, but a few deep breaths settled her wayward digestion.

She collapsed on the window seat and drew her legs up to her knees the way she had used to do when she was younger. What had possessed her to throw a book at him? She had never done anything so violent in her life before and couldn't understand why his words had so incensed her.

Neither did she know why her heart had been in her mouth when she had seen him stretched unconscious on the carpet with blood pouring down his face. Of course, to see any gentleman so struck down would have been shocking, but the fear and anguish that had gripped her was something else entirely.

She gazed unseeing from the window while she tried to make sense of what had happened. Then she relaxed as she understood why she had been so disturbed seeing Rushton injured like that. It was because she was the perpetrator of the injury, nothing else.

How long did she have before he came back and she got her comeuppance? Her maid was in the dressing room attending to some mending and must have heard the commotion, so why hadn't she come out to investigate?

'Jenny, I wish to speak to you.'

The girl appeared and curtsied politely. 'Yes, my lady.'

'I shall not be going out this evening after all, so there's no need to set out my ball gown. I shall remain in my apartment. I wish you to go down and speak to Cook; tell her to send my dinner on a tray tonight. Then I have an errand for you. Please fetch my reticule.'

Whilst her maid went for this item Giselle tried to think of something she could send the girl to buy.

'Here you are, my lady.'

'I wish you to go to the Pump Room and purchase a container of the medicinal waters. I think Lord Rushton might benefit from drinking some after his accident.' She handed over some coins and Jenny bobbed again and vanished without comment.

The last thing Rushton would want was any of the disgusting mineral water, but this was the only thing she could think of that would keep her girl away. She had no wish for anyone to overhear what was to take place between her and Rushton.

A while later there were heavy footsteps and male voices in

the passageway, which she assumed was the doctor being escorted to Rushton's rooms. She had no notion how long it would take to repair the damage, but she didn't think he would be here to punish her in less than half an hour.

This would give her ample time to change her gown, tidy her hair, and wash the tears from her face. Having been a very well-behaved child there had been no necessity for any severe punishment from her parents when they had been alive, or from Beau when he had taken over the guardianship of his family.

Of course, she had been sent to her room in disgrace, but that was the worst that had happened to her. Beau had given her the occasional tongue-lashing but he had never raised his hand to any of them.

She deserved to be beaten after what she had done and if that was what Rushton intended she would submit without protest. The more she thought about it the more agitated she became. It wasn't the thought of the pain that might be involved, it was how the procedure would take place.

Would she be tossed over his knees as if she were a child to be spanked? Would he bring his riding crop and bend her over a chair? Whatever he did, it was the embarrassment and humiliation involved rather than how much it might hurt that concerned her.

How much longer was he going to be? The sooner this was over the better. She was going mad with the waiting and the worrying. The physician had left some time ago and still he didn't come. Finally, she could bear it no longer and decided to go to him and get the matter done with.

She tumbled from the window seat, picked up her skirts and raced to his apartment. She burst in without knocking to discover him standing with his back to her, staring out of the window as she had done earlier. Her sudden entrance made him turn.

'I have come for my punishment. I have never been physically chastised before and have no idea how to go about it...'

He stared at her as if she were an inmate of an asylum gibbering rubbish. 'My dear girl, what nonsense are you saying now? I would no more raise a hand to you than I would to my daughters. Sit down, sweetheart, and we will talk about it.'

It was her turn to stare. There was a neat bandage around his forehead, his face was paler than usual, but apart from that he looked perfectly well and certainly not in a dreadful rage as she'd expected. He looked more sad than angry.

She collapsed on the *chaise longue*, which was nearest, as her legs no longer had the strength to hold her straight. 'I cannot tell you how sorry I am.'

'Can you not? I thought that was the reason you came here.'

For a moment she was puzzled by his remark and then smiled. 'I shall start again, sir. I most humbly beg your pardon...'

'No, it is I who should apologise to you. Do not look so startled, sweetheart. I had no right to behave as if I was your guardian. Only if we were genuinely betrothed should I comment on your behaviour. I had not realised just how much you resented having your name coupled with mine even on so temporary a basis. I thought we were friends...'

'We are, well you are Beau's friend, which makes you a friend of the family. Would you believe me if I said I have never thrown anything at anyone before? I am the least volatile of my siblings and yet have behaved like a hoyden these past few days. I do not understand it at all.'

He sat next to her and took her hands. Hers looked small and pale in his. 'I think we must leave here. Word of what happened will be all around the city by this evening.'

'How could that be? There was no one with us when I threw the book and as far as I was aware none of the servants were in the corridor when you fell.'

'The fact that we did not see them did not mean they were not there. We can hardly go out in public with me looking as I do.'

She removed one hand and touched his bandage gently. 'I think this makes you look romantic – like a hero from a novel who has been fighting the villain on behalf of his lady-love.' His skin was warm and for some strange reason she slid her fingers down his cheek, feeling the prickle of his bristles beneath her fingertips.

He trapped her hand beneath his and her heart skipped a beat. His eyes were dark, there was a faint flush along his cheekbones and unaccountably her bodice became too tight. Then his other hand was around her waist and she was propelled towards him.

Her breath caught in her throat. His mouth was on hers and everything changed between them.

* * *

Rushton knew he had made the most dreadful error of judgement by kissing Giselle so passionately. Even if he was genuinely betrothed to her such behaviour would still be frowned upon. Gently he removed her hands, which had become entangled in the hair at the back of his neck. Their betrothal wasn't real; he should have known better.

She smiled at him with love in her eyes and he tried to respond. She didn't understand that he could never love another woman – that a man might kiss a lady because she was desirable not because he loved her.

He was above all an honourable man, and he must somehow persuade her that he felt the same way so that she would marry him. To not do so would be despicable. His girls would be happy, and that would have to be enough for him. He would not be sharing her bed – she had made that very clear when this arrangement had been mooted. He might not be in love with her but he did want to make love to her.

'Rushton, it is as if scales have dropped from my eyes and I see you clearly for the first time. I had no idea I was in love with you until you kissed me. Was it the same for you?'

'It was indeed, my love. We have been fighting the attraction but now we can let our true feelings be known.' He dropped to one knee. 'My darling girl, will you do me the inestimable honour of becoming my wife? Will you make me the happiest of men?'

Her smile was incandescent as she nodded. He made a silent promise to himself that he would never under any circumstances allow her to know that he did not reciprocate her feeling. He found her eminently desirable, but that was not the same thing at all. Possibly having love on one side of the relationship would be sufficient to make this a happy union. He was going to do his damnedest – that was for sure.

He got to his feet and rejoined her on the daybed. 'I must speak to your brother. He will be as bewildered as we are at how quickly our plans have been changing over the past twenty-four hours. I suggest that we make arrangements to return to Hertfordshire immediately. Miss Freemantle was the instigator of this trip and she is no longer living with you. Estelle and Eloise will be content wherever they are as long as we are both with them.'

'I agree – I can see no reason for delaying our nuptials. I'm considered almost at my last prayers, so people will not be surprised that we wish to be married immediately.' She closed the distance between them and leaned into his shoulder and he had no option but to put his arm around her. She sighed and threaded her fingers through his.

'To think that my throwing the book at you revealed our true feelings. It will certainly be something to tell our children about...' She stopped and turned a delightful shade of pink.

'Do not look so discomfited, sweetheart; there is nothing you can say that will shock me. Remember, I have known you since you were in the schoolroom.'

'That is true, which means that we shall be comfortable together even though our engagement is going to be so brief.'

They sat in silence for a few minutes, she obviously enjoying being held by a gentleman for the first time in her life and he doing his best to marshal his thoughts. Silchester would be suspicious at his *volte-face* so he was the one person who must know the truth.

'Giselle, I must go and speak to your brother. Can I leave you to make the arrangements for our departure? How soon do you think you can have the luggage ready to leave?'

Immediately she was her usual, competent self. 'It can be ready to leave at first light tomorrow. However, there is one fly in this ointment, as my cousin has borrowed our carriage. The chaise belongs to this establishment and we could not travel that distance in an open vehicle anyway.'

'Dammit!' She raised an elegant eyebrow and he laughed. 'I beg your pardon, my dear, I'm afraid that I have a tendency to use inappropriate language when annoyed.'

'And I have a tendency to throw books at a person when I am annoyed. If you wish me to desist from that practice then you must desist from yours. Are we in agreement on this?'

'*Touché*, my dear. I'm at a loss to know what to do about the missing coach. Do you think Miss Freemantle will send it back?'

'I'm certain of it. She said her familial home is but three hours from here so I imagine the carriage will be back sometime tomorrow afternoon. We must allow the horses to rest for a day at least so cannot leave for three days.'

'Then we must postpone our departure until then. At least we will have ample time to send a groom to arrange for our overnight accommodation.'

She shook her head. 'They too went with my cousin. As you are *hors de combat* and cannot go out, we shall have to entertain ourselves.'

'Would you mind very much, sweetheart, if I leave tomorrow as planned? There are things that need to be done at Castlemere before I can welcome you there as my bride. It has been sadly neglected and I shall have it renewed and refurbished before you come.'

10

Rushton kissed her hand and then was gone, leaving her emotions in disarray. She swung her legs onto the daybed, stretched them out and then settled back and closed her eyes. Finally, she understood why she had been so reluctant to attend a Season, why none of the handsome young gentlemen she met had appealed to her – she had been in love with Rushton since she left the schoolroom and hadn't realised until today.

He was perfect in every detail. She could never have fallen in love with a short man, a man who did not match the superior build of her brothers. Rushton was at least two yards high, had a satisfactory breadth of shoulder, and must be the most attractive gentleman in the country.

His eyes were a strange tawny shade, which complemented his hair, which was an unusual shade somewhere between russet and gold. Others might call it mouse brown, but not her. Did Eloise inherit her blonde curls from her mother? But if so where did Estelle get her dark ringlets from? No doubt there was an ancestor they took after as they certainly didn't look like their father.

She supposed he had not declared his love to her before this as he was allowing her to be sure of her own feelings before he spoke. There was a discrepancy between their ages of more than twelve years but this was a mere bagatelle to her. She could never have been happy with a young gentleman, of that she was quite certain.

It was a great shame that Beth had gone as she would dearly like to share her happiness with her cousin. She would do her best to persuade Beau to write to Beth's mama and insist that the girl return to Silchester. She now wanted her dearest friend and cousin to be as happy as she was and decided she would write to both Lady Augusta, and her son, to see if she could perhaps move things on in that direction.

Her maid returned and handed her the water. 'There you are, my lady. I have what you asked for.'

'Thank you, Jenny. I shall be dining downstairs after all, so could you send the change of plans to the kitchen. The duke, Lord Rushton, and myself will dine together.'

Giselle picked up the glass container and recoiled in disgust at the sulphurous smell that seeped from it. One would have to be desperate to drink this and she was quite sure her beloved would not do so.

After checking that her gown was free of creases, and her hair tidy, she hurried through the house to find her brother and her future husband. They were on the terrace deep in conversation and both looked round when she approached.

'Rushton, I have a gift for you. It's the least I can do after being the cause of your injuries.' She held out the water and he took it reluctantly.

'Good God, I hope you don't expect me to drink this? I appreciate the thought, my dear; it was most kind of you.'

'I'd no idea it would smell so bad and no doubt tastes worse.'

I sent my maid to fetch it so I had to bring it down or she would have wondered why she was obliged to go to the Pump Room.'

He took it and hastily opened the lid and tipped the contents over the balustrade onto the flower border below. 'I shouldn't be surprised if the plants die, but better them than me.'

'I was intending to have a tray sent up tonight, but as it is your last night here, Rushton, I shall come down instead.' She looked enquiringly from one to the other. 'What were you two discussing so seriously? You are not going to dissuade us from marrying, Beau. It is what we both want.'

Her brother put his arm round her shoulders and hugged her. 'I am happy for you, sweetheart, and know that Rushton will make you an excellent husband. I shall send Carstairs ahead of us to arrange our accommodations and then set things in motion. I assume there is no urgency for this ceremony? You have your bride clothes to prepare and Rushton will need several weeks to refurbish Castlemere for you.'

'I should like to marry on my birthday as that way there is no danger that either of us will ever forget the date. I shall be one and twenty on the first of July, which will give you ample time to prepare things.'

'Then that is settled. Two and a half months is more than adequate.'

'I do not wish to be apart from you for so long, my love, so I implore you to return to Silchester as soon as things are put in hand. I should dearly like the girls to remain with me if you would agree? I wish to get to know them better.'

'Of course they can remain at Silchester with their governess. I give you my word, my dear, that I will be no longer than is necessary. Do you care to ride with me?'

As she was considering her response something else occurred to her. 'You cannot travel all the way to Essex on horseback, Rushton, when you have six stitches and a bandage on your head. Do not you agree, Beau?'

'Now that you mention it, I think you are correct, Giselle. Better to travel by post-chaise, my friend, despite the exorbitant cost of so doing.'

She was about to suggest that he travelled in the carriage with her but realised there would be no room for him to do this. Her brother would be obliged to ride as well, but he didn't have a head wound so there would be no danger for him.

Again, the two gentlemen exchanged glances – there was something going on between them that she was not privy to. 'I have another suggestion to put to both of you. Why do not we travel together? If we break it into easy stages then your mounts will not be too tired to continue the next day and neither will the carriage horses. Carstairs could arrange for us to stay in attractive places each night. If we curtail our travelling to a few hours only, I think it will be more enjoyable for all of us.'

She waited for a response but they both seemed reluctant to commit themselves to her excellent plan. 'I can see no harm in you riding for only a few hours each day, Rushton, so your injury will be no handicap then. You have well over two months to set things in motion, my love. I'm sure that a few days more will make no difference.'

'Very well, I shall not leave tomorrow but wait and travel with you to Silchester. I shall see my girls settled and get your local physician to remove my stitches. It is a shame that my own carriage will already have returned to Castlemere, but it seemed the sensible option at the time to send it back.'

The matter satisfactorily sorted Giselle pointed to the garden where the children were playing a lively game of cricket with their governess. 'I'm going to join in – I think both of you should do so as well. That way we can have equal teams.'

Rushton laughed. 'I must not ride, according to your strictures, sweetheart, but it will be perfectly acceptable for me to rush about the place after a cricket ball.'

'The difference is, as you very well know, sir, that if anything untoward was to happen you will be attended to at once.'

'Then I am happy to comply and you have no option but to do the same, Silchester.'

* * *

He would have preferred to join Estelle and Miss Gibbons, and leave Giselle and her brother and Eloise to make up the other team, but he thought this might seem odd to his future wife. They spent an enjoyable interlude playing until the governess declared it was time for nursery tea. His children curtsied politely to the duke and himself but threw their arms around Giselle's neck.

There was still an hour before he needed to change for dinner but he had no wish to spend it with either Giselle or her brother. He complained he had a headache and rubbed his eyes to make his words seem more genuine.

'It is my fault – I should never have asked you to play. You must retire immediately and rest. I'll get Cook to make you a soothing tisane.'

'There's no need for that, sweetheart. A rest is all that is needed.'

She walked beside him, her arm pushed through his until they reached the stairs where they parted. She went into the study with her brother, no doubt to discuss wedding plans whilst he made his way to his apartment.

This was a damnable business. He was torn by conflicting emotions, not sure whether marrying a girl who loved him when he could not reciprocate or... what? There was no alternative to marrying her – and he could never reveal his true feelings.

Silchester had been sympathetic but told him in no uncertain terms that the marriage would take place. He had also been warned that if ever she discovered there was love on only one side of the union he would answer to the duke.

Rushton couldn't be bothered to remove his boots as that would mean calling his valet to assist him. Penrose would come when it was time to change for dinner; until then he would lie on the bed as he was, with boots and jacket on.

Marrying for love was the exception rather than the rule and he was certain that many men in his position had taken a bride when their feelings were no more than lukewarm. More often than not status and money were what mattered to both the man and the woman.

Giselle would be a wonderful mother to his children and to any other babies they might produce together. Having a son from the union would be a bonus indeed. His lips curved as he reviewed what he was gaining from this marriage.

She was as kind and intelligent as she was beautiful. It would be no hardship making love to her and he was confident she would never be aware that it was passion and not love that they shared in the marital bed.

That she would also bring a substantial dowry to the marriage made no difference to him. He had more than enough in his coffers and had no need of any further funds. Therefore, he had insisted the dowry would remain hers to use as she wished and would not be absorbed into his estate.

His valet woke him from his slumber and tutted under his breath at seeing his master fully clothed on the bed. Rushton was ready in good time so decided to slip upstairs and speak to his girls before he went down to join the others in the drawing room.

The girls were sprawled on the carpet playing a noisy game of spillikins but jumped up and ran to join him as he strolled in. 'Papa, we are so excited that you and Mama are to be married in July and not wait until next year as we thought,' Estelle said.

Hearing her call Giselle mama was too much, too soon. 'She is not your mama, and until we are wed you will refer to her as Aunt Giselle. Do I make myself quite clear?'

They stepped away from him, their faces shocked by his sharp remark and he wished the words unsaid. Too late for regrets, the damage was done. 'I came to tell you that you will not be leaving until the carriage returns. His grace and I are now going to accompany you on the journey and we intend to take it slowly so we don't have to change horses.'

This news was enough to restore their happy smiles. 'It will be an adventure, Papa, and we don't mind how long it takes as long as we don't have to spend more than a few hours each day shut up in a smelly old carriage.' Estelle looked at her sister for confirmation and Eloise nodded vigorously.

'Miss Gibbons, I hope you are happy to remain in my employ when we leave Bath?'

The governess bobbed. 'Yes, my lord, I am delighted to stay with these girls. I can tell you with absolute honesty that I have never been so happy in my life as I am right now. Lady Giselle is so considerate of my feelings that it is has been a pleasure to work for her.'

'You will remain at Silchester Court with my daughters until Lady Giselle and I are wed. Then we shall all return to Castlemere.'

This encounter left him with a sour taste in his mouth. If he wasn't to alienate his darling daughters he must accept the inevitable and force himself to be happy about his forthcoming marriage when he was the reverse.

'I apologise for my tardiness, Giselle, Silchester, but I went up to say goodnight to my girls.'

The footman glided to his side with a silver tray upon which were glasses of champagne. Reluctantly he took one – he didn't feel in a celebratory mood but he must appear to be happy if he wasn't to destroy the girl who deserved better than a loveless union.

'I raise my glass to you both, and wish you every happiness in the future.' The duke drained his glass and took a second.

'Thank you for your good wishes, Beau. I intend for us to be as happy as my siblings. My only regret is that I shall be living so far away from Silchester when everyone else is within an hour's drive.'

This was something he could reassure her about. 'You shall visit whenever you wish to, sweetheart, and your family can come to Castlemere.'

Her smile was radiant. 'Thank you, I knew you would understand. I have something I must tell you both before we go in to dine. I wish to write to Beth and ask her to return to us. I owe my happiness to her, for if she hadn't attempted to run away Rushton and I would not have discovered our feelings for each other.'

'Then by all means have her back, Giselle,' Beau said. 'I warn you that it will take me some time to forgive her, so she had best keep out of my way.'

'She might be silly but she is not stupid, Beau; she will avoid you. Silchester is so vast one could go a month without meeting another occupant if that's what one wished.

'You are the kindest of brothers. I shall have the letter sent tomorrow morning. Our cousin can assist in the planning of my wedding and help me prepare my bride clothes. Although I have little need for more gowns as I replenished my wardrobe before we came here.'

The butler announced that dinner was served and Rushton held out his arm for her to place hers through. Silchester took the lead, leaving them to walk together. 'You are quiet this evening. Is there something bothering you?' Giselle asked.

'I apologise if I have seemed distracted, my love, but my head is full of what needs doing at your future home. The more I think about it, the more I realise how neglected the interior of the house has become.'

'I would be quite happy to move in as it is, Rushton, and then be able to have some say in the redecoration and improvements.'

Her suggestion made sense. 'In which case, sweetheart, I shall just have your apartment done and we will make decisions about everything else together. Do you have any preference for style or colour?'

'I am not overfond of the Egyptian look, which has been fashionable. I have a preference for pale colours and the furniture of Chippendale. However, I shall be satisfied with whatever is there. I have no intention of being a demanding bride.'

'I, however, shall be an accommodating husband and your wish shall be my command.'

Her laugh echoed down the passageway. 'And I, sir, shall sprout wings and fly if that proves to be the case.'

11

SILCHESTER COURT, JUNE 1814

'Is that a letter from Rushton, Giselle?' Beth asked.

'It is, yet another delay. I cannot believe that he has remained away from me all these weeks with only a weekly letter to sustain me. One would have thought his home was falling down judging by the amount of time it has taken him to put things right.'

'You have the rest of your life to spend together, dearest, so what do a few weeks apart matter? Lady Augusta has invited me to visit after the wedding. I think she has finally accepted that her son and I are destined to be together whatever the obstacles.'

Giselle smiled. 'I rather think that her change of heart, my dear, came when she realised your provenance and the fact that you are so rich an heiress.'

'I don't care what it was, as long as one day Theodore and I shall be man and wife. I have received more letters from him than you have received from your betrothed, and he is stationed somewhere on the Peninsula, not living in Essex.'

'Do you know when he might be able to get leave so you can become officially engaged?'

'Lady Augusta tells me that might not be for years – but I am prepared to wait. His duty to King and Country must come before his love for me.' Her cousin spoilt this noble statement by giggling. 'We have plans that I cannot tell you, but they do not involve us being apart.'

'My brother is keeping a watchful eye on you, Beth, so if you are thinking of running away a second time I should think again.'

'You have no need to fret; I shall do nothing that will scandalise the family. In fact, I'm hoping I will have the approval of one member at least.'

There was no opportunity to question her cousin further as the girls called to her from the terrace. She had promised to join in a treasure hunt that Miss Gibbons had organised. The only benefit to her having been left without the man she adored at her side was that she had been able to spend part of every day with her soon-to-be daughters. They were now calling her mama and she loved them as if they were her own children.

When the final clue was solved, all four of them were grubby and in need of refreshments. 'Mama,' Estelle said, 'why has Papa not come back as he promised?'

'You know why, my love: he has been kept busy with estate business. In the letter I received today he said he is setting out in two days' time and will be here the day before our marriage.'

'Can we attend the ball, Mama? We will be very quiet.'

'No, Eloise, you may not. However, I shall ask Miss Gibbons to let you watch from the gallery for a while. You have the garden party to look forward to the next day. This event has become a tradition to follow a Sheldon marriage.'

'Why is it a Sheldon marriage, and not a Silchester marriage, Mama?'

'Our family name is Sheldon – Uncle Bennett as you know is called Lord Sheldon. The dukedom is Silchester.'

By the time she had finished her explanation Eloise had lost interest and was already chattering to the governess about the prizes they had acquired during the treasure hunt.

Beau was dining out so she and Beth would eat upstairs. Despite the reassurances she had received in Rushton's loving letters she was becoming more concerned by the day that there was something amiss. When she had asked her brother, he had dismissed her fears as those of a young lady anxious about becoming a married woman.

Her older sister, Madeline, had explained to her what was involved when a husband and wife shared the marital bed. The whole thing sounded quite extraordinary, but she was assured that after some initial discomfort, intimacy between her and Rushton would be pleasurable.

Her bride clothes were packed in tissue paper in trunks and the gown she was to wear for the ceremony was laid out on a shelf in her closet. On the shelf below was the ball gown she would change into that evening and the ensemble she would wear at the garden party.

She wasn't sure if she was relieved or concerned when her brother had explained she was to remain in her own apartment until she and her husband left Silchester. No doubt it would be more comfortable for all concerned if she remained pure until she was in her own home. At least that was one thing she did not have to worry about initially.

The girls scarcely remembered their mother as she had died when Estelle had been five and Eloise three. Beau had told her very little about the first Lady Rushton apart from the fact that they had both been very young and childhood sweethearts.

*　*　*

As the time for his arrival drew closer, she slept less – and when she did, her dreams were troubled and she awoke as tired as she had been when she had closed her eyes. There were so many things he had not given her the opportunity to ask. Would the staff accept her as the mistress or were they still loyal to his first wife? Were they to take a wedding trip or remain at Castlemere? Did they have a church in the grounds or did they attend the one in the village? Was he familiar with his neighbours? Would there be ladies of a similar age to her that she could become acquainted with?

She was up at dawn on the day he was due to come and decided to take her mare out for an early morning ride to clear her head. The aroma of summer blooms greeted her as she descended the stairs. Everywhere she looked there were huge vases of both hothouse and garden flowers. Only the family were to attend the ceremony and the wedding breakfast; their neighbours and friends were to come to the ball that evening to celebrate their nuptials.

After an invigorating gallop she returned to the house to find her brother waiting to speak to her. Her heart sunk to her boots. 'What is it? Has Rushton met with an accident on his way here?'

'No, sweetheart, nothing so bad. An annoyance, no more than that. I have just received a letter by express from him saying he was unavoidably delayed again but will be here in time for the ceremony tomorrow.'

Her eyes filled. There was only one conclusion she could

draw from his absence, he did not wish to marry her. 'I think the wedding should be cancelled. I've no wish to marry a man who doesn't love me.'

'I'm sure that is not the reason he has been delayed again. He will reassure you of his feelings when he arrives. I will not force you into something you do not want, but before you insist on this, I'm afraid there is something you should see.' He took her arm and guided her into the drawing room then handed her a copy of *The Times*. It was already open at a news story that made her stomach curdle.

The article referred to her and Rushton by initials only but it was obvious to her and anyone else upon whom the scandal was being directed. Word of their early morning escapade had somehow been sent to this paper, no doubt by the butler at the establishment they had rented, and it made her sound as if she was little better than a lady of the night. Rushton was depicted as a gentleman of low morals. They had no option but to tie the knot – it was the only way the good name of both families could be restored.

'I can see I have no option but to continue. Tomorrow was to be the happiest day of my life and now it will be the worst.' She couldn't continue; if she did she would disgrace herself by breaking down.

Instead of an intimate family dinner with her brother, her cousin and her future husband she dined alone in her sitting room and retired early, long before it got dark, too miserable to remain on her feet. She fell into a fitful doze to be woken by what she thought were voices on the terrace below. Surely one of them was Rushton and the other her brother?

* * *

'I don't give a damn how you do it, Rushton, but you will convince my sister you are neck over crop in love with her or I won't answer for the consequences. Any other man in the kingdom would be overjoyed to be marrying her – she is beautiful, intelligent, the sister of a duke and a substantial heiress. What is the matter with you, for God's sake?'

'She deserves better than me, Silchester. I shall not cavil if she wants to break the engagement. She loves me but I cannot reciprocate her feelings. To be marrying again seems like a betrayal of the love I had for my first wife...' He flinched as Silchester clenched his fist. 'She will get over me, find herself someone who can love her.'

The duke shoved a newspaper into his hand and as he read the article he knew that this meant that even if she wished to jilt him she could no longer do so. The marriage must go ahead as planned. He had stayed away from her hoping she would change her mind, realise that she could do better than him, and this had been the case. But now, because of this article, he must do his best to make her happy.

'When she came back she was radiant but as the days have passed without your appearance here she has faded before my eyes – you will be shocked at how much weight she has lost and how her hair has lost its lustre. Your daughters adore her and are already calling her mama – that is reason enough for you to be happy about the union.'

'It is not yet midnight. I shall go up and speak to her, convince her that I haven't changed my mind. Do I have your permission to enter her bedchamber?'

'I think that horse has bolted as far as the world is concerned. Do what you must. I expect to see her smiling as my brother Bennett walks her down the aisle. I hope we understand each other?'

Silchester was his groomsman so couldn't escort his sister as he ought, but his brother would make an excellent substitute.

Rushton made his way to her apartment and tapped on her bedchamber door. There was no answer. He could hardly knock louder, not while standing in the corridor as he was. This was not the sensible way to organise things; he would do better to enter through the sitting room.

The door from this room was ajar. He pushed it open and saw at once she was awake and sitting up in bed. 'Giselle, my darling, I have come to explain why I have stayed away from you these past weeks.' There was no answer. Her face was indistinct in the darkness and he didn't think it would be polite to move closer.

'I knew if I was here I would be unable to stay out of your bed – I would have pre-empted our wedding night and that was something I could not do to you. I should not be here now. Your brother would run me through if he discovered me...'

The shape moved and she flew across the room and into his arms. Every inch of her body was pressed against him. Her breasts were soft, her skin smooth and hot. For the first time in years his passion rose and he swept her up, kicked the door shut behind him and carried her to her bed.

'I love you so much, I have been beside myself with misery these past weeks. Why did you not tell me the reason you were staying from me?'

His heart was pounding; his wits were scattered. All he could think about was removing her nightgown and his clothes as speedily as possible.

'I thought that your brother might read your letters first. We should not be doing this – we should wait until tomorrow.' Even to him his voice sounded different but she was undeterred.

'We are damned by the gossips so we might as well do what they said we have already done.'

She was untying his neckcloth as she spoke and having her fingers brushing his neck was adding to the desire inflaming his senses. From somewhere he found the strength to pull back. He didn't dare to kiss her although it was killing him to keep his mouth from hers. If he did he would not be able to stop and they would both regret it in the morning.

'Darling, I have never wanted anything so much as to make you mine – but I will not do it until we are man and wife. This must wait until tomorrow.' He moved a safe distance from her, knowing his resolve was weak and it wouldn't take much to make him change his mind.

'There is the wedding breakfast, then a ball, which will go on until the small hours...'

'Which means we have the entire afternoon to ourselves. Dismiss your maid and I shall spend those hours showing you just how much I love you.'

'That sounds quite delightful and impossibly daring. You must go now. I shall sleep for the first time in weeks now I know that you love me as much as I love you, and that tomorrow we will begin our life together.'

'Good night, sweetheart.' He closed the door behind him and left feeling happier than he had done since he had been forced to offer for her. Desire was not the same as love, but it was second best. If he could keep her happy in the bedroom then she would not notice there was something missing in their relationship. Once she had babies of her own she would have no time to think about this and would enjoy what she had.

He had made good use of the intervening weeks and his home was now ready to receive the new Lady Rushton. The kitchens had been moved so that in future food would arrive in the dining room hot, which would be a great improvement. He'd also had installed a bathing room attached to her apartment, which he was sure she would appreciate.

The entire establishment had been freshly painted, hand-printed wallpaper in fashionable green and gold stripes had been applied to the walls in the drawing room, and fresh curtains had been made and were hanging in place in all the main reception rooms. Even the girls' domain had been updated and the small apartment Miss Gibbons would occupy was now greatly improved.

He'd had no intention of speaking to his host again but Silchester was waiting for him in his sitting room. 'Well, have you put matters right between you?'

'I have. Although this is not an auspicious start, I give you my word as a gentleman I shall make your sister happy and she will never know the truth.'

'Good man. Many a happy marriage starts with far less than you two have. It scarcely matters, if you want my opinion, if you love her or not as long as you are fond of her, and do not find her boring company.'

'She will be a lively companion and the perfect mother for my girls and any children we might have together. I'm taking her directly to Castlemere after the garden party as I wish her to see the improvements I have made and become familiar with her home. Then I shall take her on an extended tour of the north whilst the weather is clement.

'I expect to be returning south in September and will come here for an extended stay before returning permanently to Castlemere. Would it be in order to invite Miss Gibbons and the girls to return to Silchester then?'

'Of course. I am away to my bed, my friend, and I suggest you do the same.'

Surprisingly, Rushton slept soundly and awoke the next morning eager to make Giselle his second wife. She would never mean the same to him as his beloved Charlotte but he had never expected to love another woman as he had done his first wife. As Silchester had pointed out to him, more marriages were based on status and money than they were on romantic love.

* * *

'There, my lady, you look a picture. Jonquil muslin was a perfect choice for your wedding gown. The spencer in a darker shade of yellow complements it as it should.' Jenny stepped back to admire her handiwork. 'At what time do you wish me to return to prepare you for the ball?'

'I shall ring for you. On no account must you return to my apartment until then.' Giselle knew her maid would know exactly why she was banned for the afternoon and her cheeks coloured.

The sound of childish laughter alerted her to the arrival of her daughters; they were to be flower girls and scatter rose petals down the aisle in front of her as she walked to join her future husband at the altar.

'Mama, your gown is so pretty. I shall have one exactly the same when I get married,' Estelle announced.

'I shall too,' her sister chimed in.

Miss Gibbons was wearing an elegant gown and looked almost pretty. The governess was obviously much younger than Giselle had at first thought. 'Come along, girls, we must collect your basket of petals so you are waiting when her ladyship appears on the arm of Lord Sheldon.'

'Did someone mention my name?' Her brother Bennett appeared at the door resplendent in a bottle green jacket, light green silk waistcoat and an intricate frothy white neckcloth held in place by single diamond stick pin.

Miss Gibbons curtsied as did the girls and then they hurried away, leaving her alone with him. 'Is it time? I thought there was another half an hour before the ceremony.'

'Everyone is in the chapel including Rushton. Whatever Beau has said to you, sweetheart, it's not too late to change your mind. Better to have scandal attached to your name than live unhappily the rest of your life.'

She reached up and kissed his cheek, having to stand on tiptoes to do so. 'I love him to distraction. I believe I have always done so ever since I was a young girl. I cannot wait to be his wife and he is as eager as I to tie the knot.'

Bennett held out his arm and she slipped hers through it. 'You look quite beautiful, little sister, and I can see from your expression how happy you are. I think that Rushton did the right thing giving you space to change your mind even though you found it hard to bear.'

'He would never do anything to hurt me deliberately. He is an honourable gentleman – and prodigiously handsome, don't you think?'

* * *

The ceremony was conducted but she was scarcely aware of what took place. He spoke when asked and before she knew it she was a bride and her husband was slipping a gold band over her knuckle. His wicked smile sent shivers of anticipation down her spine.

It was customary for the groom to kiss the bride and she had expected to receive a chaste kiss on her cheek. He had other ideas entirely and she was crushed against his chest whilst his mouth closed over hers. When eventually he raised his head she was hot all over and incandescent with excitement and happiness.

'Lord Rushton, Lady Giselle, would you care to lead the way down the aisle so we may go to the dining room for the wedding breakfast.' Beau sounded amused rather than horrified at their immodest display.

As there was only family present, it seemed silly to stand on ceremony. She ran and embraced her sister Madeline and her brother-in-law Lord Carshalton, then she did the same for Grace, Bennett's lovely wife. Finally, she hugged her cousin and was then ready to promenade from the chapel on her husband's arm.

12

The wedding breakfast seemed interminable and Giselle was obliged to eat and drink far more than she was accustomed to in the middle of the day. After three glasses of champagne she stopped worrying about what was going to happen when she left the table and began to enjoy herself.

Eventually the meal drew to a close and the party dispersed. They would all meet again at eight o'clock that evening. She had quite forgotten it was her birthday as well as her wedding day, and so apparently had everybody else as no one had thought to congratulate her on becoming one and twenty.

Her head was spinning a little and she was obliged to steady herself by gripping the back of the chair as she turned to leave the dining room. She hadn't dared to look at her husband in case by so doing she revealed what they were planning to do for the remainder of the afternoon.

The girls, who had been allowed to eat with them as this was a special occasion, trotted off obediently with their governess, leaving her free to make her way to her apartment. She wished she had not dismissed Jenny before she had been helped out of her wedding gown, for there were too many bows and buttons to undo especially as her fingers refused to answer her commands.

She wasn't sure if she should put on her nightgown, stay in her undergarments or remain as she was and allow her husband to remove everything that was necessary. The bed looked inviting so she thought she would take a nap while she waited for him to join her.

Being flat was an unpleasant experience as she felt as if she was in a boat being rocked violently from side to side. She closed her eyes and that made things a little better. The next thing she knew she was being shaken by the shoulder by her maid.

'My lady, I waited and waited for you to ring but then thought I had better come up as you have barely an hour to get ready for the ball.'

Giselle clutched her hands to her mouth, tumbled out bed and grabbed the chamber pot before she cast up her accounts. After several unpleasant minutes she sat back, her face clammy, her head pounding. 'I am not at all well. I cannot go down again today. You must immediately send a message to Lord Rushton and explain I'm indisposed. He will apologise to the duke and our guests on my behalf.'

'I shall help you out of your gown, my lady, and into bed before I take the message.'

With the bed hangings closed around her and the shutters closed, the room was pleasantly dark. She could not imagine how she could have been so unlucky as to eat something that disagreed with her so violently on her wedding day.

Jenny returned with a soothing tisane from Cook, which settled her stomach and made her feel a little less dizzy. She sincerely hoped she would feel more herself the following morning as she did not wish to miss the garden party as well as the ball.

* * *

Rushton watched his wife totter from the room and cursed under his breath. He should have stopped her drinking so much – she wasn't used to alcohol. He had bought her a pretty emerald necklace for her birthday and had intended to give it to her when he went to her in her bedchamber.

He smiled ruefully when he saw his wife passed out on the bed. Consummating the union would have to wait until they got back to Castlemere as this was the only opportunity they had to be private until then.

There was paper, a decent pen and ink on her bureau and he quickly scribbled her a note and then put his gift on top of it. He placed it on the mantelshelf where he was sure she would find it when she eventually awoke.

The house was quiet, the guests had departed for their own homes to return later. Where Silchester was he had no idea, but thought perhaps it was better not to spend time alone with his brother-in-law in case he revealed the true state of affairs. One could spend only so much time admiring the floral decorations before becoming bored.

He had expected to spend the afternoon making love to his wife and so was now full of pent-up energy and frustration. He bounded back to his apartment and his valet helped him change into his riding gear. He would gallop about the countryside until it was time to return and change for the ball.

After spending an enjoyable few hours he returned to the stable yard and hurried inside. He was immediately accosted by the butler.

An Accommodating Husband

'My lord, I received a message a while ago that Lady Giselle is indisposed and will not be able to attend the ball. I have informed his grace of this fact.'

This was a damnable nuisance as it was going to look rather odd if the happy couple were not there to be congratulated. No doubt there would be some attending the event who would erroneously assume that they had already fallen out with each other – or even worse – that she was suffering from the sickness associated with being in an interesting condition.

However unwell she felt, it was caused by alcohol, nothing else. He would insist that she pulled herself together, got ready, and came down to greet the guests.

He should have knocked before entering her sitting room but was too agitated to wait for someone to come to the door. Her maid appeared and curtsied nervously.

'Lady Giselle is asleep, my lord. She has been very unwell.'

'She is not ill, but suffering from the effects of too much alcohol this morning. Out of my way – I'm going to speak to her myself. Get her gown out and everything else that she needs. My wife will be getting dressed and attending the ball as planned.'

He strode to the bed and threw back the hangings. Without waiting for her to argue he lifted her from between the sheets and placed her on her feet. 'Get yourself washed and dressed at once. I will brook no disobedience – I am your husband and you will do as I say. Do I make myself clear?'

For a moment she stared as if she didn't recognise him, then her lips thinned and her eyes narrowed. 'Very well, my lord, if you insist. Kindly remove yourself whilst I get dressed.' She sniffed audibly and pulled a face of displeasure. 'I do not take kindly to being roused by a gentleman smelling of the stable.'

She stepped away from him, turned her back and stalked into the dressing room. The door was closed firmly behind her.

He had been given his marching orders and he deserved no less. What had he been thinking to barge in like this and issue orders? He had treated her like a recalcitrant schoolgirl and he didn't blame her one jot for taking umbrage.

There was no point giving his gift to her now, not when she was in this mood. He put the box with the necklace into his pocket and left his wife to her ablutions. It took him longer than he would have liked to remove the smell of the stable from his person and get into his evening rig.

At least one of them should be down to greet the guests. He hurtled down the staircase to find Giselle ahead of him, already standing in line with the duke ready to greet the first arrivals who were just entering through the open front door.

Apart from appearing paler than usual, his wife looked quite beautiful. She was wearing a stunning confection that one minute appeared to be gold and the next silver. The bodice clung to her curves and the skirts moved as she did.

'Good evening, my lord – you are tardy. I have been here this age anticipating your appearance.' She spoke quietly so her brother could not hear her sharp words.

His admiration turned instantly to anger. 'It is not your place to correct my behaviour, madam. You would be wise to remember that.'

She ignored his reprimand and turned to smile at the couple at the head of the queue. Countless strangers were introduced to him but he forgot their names as soon as they were a few yards from him. They were to start the dancing as the ball was to celebrate their nuptials.

The orchestra had been squealing and squeaking like dying cats for the past half an hour so he must assume they were now ready to begin and were just awaiting the arrival of himself and his partner.

An Accommodating Husband

All the guests were now inside. He didn't hold out his arm as he feared she would refuse to put a hand on it. Instead he reached down and took her hand instead. She was of course wearing evening gloves – he refused to put on the wretched things himself. He had recovered his temper long ago but she still remained aloof.

'They are expecting us, sweetheart, as the proceedings cannot start until we are there to open them.'

She smiled, but it did not reach her eyes. 'I shall dance with you twice, as is expected, and then once each with my brothers and then I shall retire. I do not expect you to visit my apartment tonight or any other night. Do I make myself clear?'

This repetition of the phrase he had used to her earlier was deliberate. He should be glad she did not require his attentions, did not appear to hold him in affection any longer, but for some reason he was devastated at her rejection and he could not understand why this should be.

* * *

Giselle's anger at her husband's callous treatment had enabled her to remain upright whilst Jenny prepared her for the evening. She was ready in half the usual time and determined to be down before he came to collect her. As she had a few minutes to spare she wandered around her sitting room and spied a note on her mantelpiece. She did not recognise the writing. She broke the seal and spread out the paper.

Giselle,

I had not forgotten it was your birthday today and have bought you a small gift. I hope that you like it.

Your loving husband

There was nothing with the envelope. He had obviously decided not to give it to her because of her impertinence. How had things come to this so quickly? This morning she had been so happy she thought she would burst and now was in the depths of despair. She had married someone she no longer recognised. Until today he had been unfailingly polite, accommodating and affectionate, but all this had changed as soon as she had his ring on her finger.

Perhaps dismissing him from her bedchamber had not been a wise thing to do but it was too late to recant – the words were said and the rift had occurred. She was not going to be the one to apologise; it should be him. She would remain apart from him for as long as it took as she was adamant she would not become a subservient and browbeaten wife.

She pinched her cheeks in an attempt to make them pinker but failed – the aftermath of her overindulgence she was sure, and it served her right. In future, she would be more careful how much she imbibed.

'The gold silk underskirt, my lady, looks a treat underneath the silver sparkles. Are you sure you don't wish to wear any of your jewellery tonight?'

'No, the gown is lovely enough as it is. I do not intend to remain above an hour or two so I shall require you at ten o'clock.'

Beau was waiting for her. He looked magnificent in his black. He was by far the handsomest of her brothers even though they were all attractive gentlemen. It was a great shame he had set his mind against marrying, for he would make a lucky young lady a wonderful husband.

'You look quite enchanting, little sister. I thought you would have come down with Rushton as you spent the afternoon together.'

Her face turned an unbecoming shade of red and she couldn't meet his glance. 'I was unwell, and needed to sleep. I shall never drink champagne again; that is for certain.'

He chuckled. 'That is a lesson we have all learned, but I am sorry you had to find out today that too much alcohol is not good for one. Ah! I can hear our first guests – I hope Rushton is not much longer or there will be talk.' He kissed her gently on the cheek. 'By the way, I had not forgotten it is your anniversary today. I thought to give you a joint wedding gift and birthday gift. You will discover what it is tomorrow.'

There was no time to enquire further as she was obliged to smile and accept the congratulations of the first arrivals. Rushton appeared at her side and she couldn't resist a sharp comment. His response was angry and immediate. She pretended not to hear. Although not well versed in the ways of married couples, she knew enough to understand that even the most loving partners had occasional arguments. She thought it unlikely that anyone genuinely in love with their partner would fall out with them so soon after the knot was tied.

When he led her to the ballroom she forced a smile and prayed that nobody knew it wasn't genuine. He was an excellent dancer and if she hadn't felt so wretched she would have enjoyed the experience. When she had completed the four dances she had decided she would perform – two of them with her husband – she slipped away without bidding anyone goodnight.

Jenny undressed her in silence and for that she was grateful. She had no wish to make idle chit-chat tonight. She put on her usual nightgown, one of white cotton with lace at throat and sleeves, not the fine lawn sleeveless item that had been made for her wedding night. If her maid thought this strange she cared not.

As soon as she was alone she hurried to the sitting room door and pushed the back of a chair under the doorknob. This would prevent him from entering. There was a bolt on the bedchamber door that exited onto the passageway and she pushed this across. The only way her husband could come in was if he took the servants' staircase and entered through the dressing room. Only the family knew the way through the rabbit warren of passages – he would become hopelessly lost if he attempted this.

Her head was thumping and the all too familiar pain over her left eye heralded the start of one of her sick headaches. Once a megrim set in she was often incapacitated for several days and she prayed this wouldn't be the case this time. She had already caused enough upset and drama and sincerely wished to attend the garden party and be well enough to depart the following morning for her marital home.

As she had eaten nothing since she had cast up her accounts earlier, the nausea was not as bad. It was as if someone was banging a nail through her eye and at times like these she wished she could take laudanum to ease the pain. Beau had never allowed her to do this so she must suffer until it lifted.

Beau was well aware how ill she became and would, hopefully, placate her husband so he would be sympathetic rather than irate.

13

Rushton was standing on the terrace watching the activity on the vast expanse of grass when his host wandered out to speak to him.

'There you are; I've been searching for you. I'm sorry to tell you that Giselle has one of her occasional megrims. Once she is stricken thus she is unable to rise from her bed for sometimes as much as three days. She will not be coming to the garden party and will not be able to leave tomorrow as planned.'

For a moment Rushton thought this was a prevarication, but then pushed this thought aside. 'She will be sad to miss this event, for I know she has been looking forward to seeing the stilt-walkers, fire-eaters and other things that have been planned. How often does she suffer from these sick headaches?'

'Fortunately, only a handful of times a year. I'm certain this has been triggered by her overindulgence in alcohol yesterday.'

'I think I shall leave as planned tomorrow, take my girls and the governess home and then return to collect my wife when she is well. I'm sure she will not wish to be cooped up for hours in a carriage, with two lively children, after having been so unwell. I thought that I could drive her to Castlemere myself. Your wedding and birthday gifts of matching chestnuts and a chaise has to be taken, so why not combine the two?'

'An excellent notion, my friend. My sister will enjoy travelling in an open carriage with you – let's hope the weather remains fine as the hood is more for decoration than purpose.'

'I should like to speak to her before I go. Is she likely to be well enough to receive visitors by tomorrow morning?'

'Unlikely. I suggest that you write her a note explaining why you have left without her. She would not thank you for a visit when she is so poorly.'

With that Rushton had to be satisfied. It was not an ideal start to their marriage, but once they were at his home he would woo her in earnest. He wanted her to feel loved before he made love to her.

His girls were disappointed their new mama was unable to join them in the festivities but they still enjoyed themselves and so did he. He rather thought, if Giselle approved, he would arrange something similar for his tenants, villagers and neighbours. There had been nothing to celebrate since his beloved Charlotte had died so suddenly but now there was. He had a lovely young wife to show off and he was determined to do so.

He dined quietly in his room as they were to set off at dawn. As he trimmed his quill to write the letter he remembered he had left the previous one on the mantelshelf but had taken away the gift. He smacked his forehead with his hand, splattering ink across his cheek and down the wallpaper.

His language turned the air blue and he heard his valet chuckling in the other room. Small wonder she had been frosty with him; she must have thought he had taken away the gift deliberately when that was the last thing he intended.

He was going to have to do a deal of grovelling to put this right.

Dearest Giselle,

I am so sorry that you have missed so much of our celebrations because of ill health. I believe that I may have been the cause of some of this upset and give you my word as a gentleman that I will make it up to you when we are home together.

You should not have had that letter without the gift. I didn't realise I had left it behind. Here's the necklace I bought you for your birthday – I wanted to give it to you when you were well, not when you were feeling the effects of too much champagne.

I hope you are soon well as I hate to think of you so sick. I am taking the girls back tomorrow, but will then return to collect you. I cannot tell you how we will be travelling – you must speak to your brother about that as it is a surprise from him.

Once you are settled at Castlemere I thought we might hold a ball and a garden party to celebrate our nuptials and for you to meet our tenants, villagers and neighbours. It is something we can talk about on the drive home.

Your baggage will be transported as planned and both your maid and my valet will go with it and see that everything is unpacked satisfactorily.

I don't believe I told you how beautiful you looked at the ball. You must wear that ensemble for our own event as I don't believe I've ever seen anything quite so lovely as you were when you wore it.

I am counting the hours until we can be together again,
Your loving husband

He scrawled his signature, sanded the paper, folded and sealed it by pressing his ring into the blob of molten wax. A light tap on her sitting room door elicited an immediate response. The door opened and her maid curtsied.

'How is my wife? Is she any better?'

'She is not, my lord, but will be fully recovered in a day or two.'

'I wish you to give her these as soon as she is well enough to receive them. Also, you will be leaving tomorrow with the luggage and his grace has arranged for someone else to take care of your mistress until she is well enough to travel herself.'

'Yes, my lord, I shall see that she gets them.' The girl bobbed again and he returned to his apartment, satisfied he had done all he could for the moment to repair the damage he had inadvertently caused.

* * *

After an extremely unpleasant two days Giselle thought she was ready to rise from her bed, put on her bedrobe and go into the sitting room. She rang for Jenny but another girl appeared in answer to her summons.

'Where is my maid?'

The girl dipped and smiled. 'She has gone ahead, my lady. I am to take care of you until you are well enough to travel yourself.'

Although somewhat shocked by this announcement, she realised it made sense, and she supposed she could not have been consulted as she was too ill to receive visitors.

'Could you inform my husband that I will receive him when it is convenient for him to come?'

'His lordship and the girls left yesterday, my lady.'

An Accommodating Husband

She was too dispirited to answer. He had deserted her. He could not have made his feelings plainer. Whatever he had said, he had married her because he was an honourable man, not because he loved her as he professed to.

'I'm going to remain in bed. I don't wish to be disturbed. I shall ring when I want you.' She sank back on the pillows. 'Close the hangings and shutters again, please.'

Once she was private she let the tears flow and her pillow was sodden before she eventually fell asleep. Then someone was shaking her none too gently.

'Wake up, you goose. He has not abandoned you – you are making yourself unhappy for no reason.' Beau dragged her upright and rammed a couple of pillows behind her back. He then flung back the hangings and banged the shutters open.

'Read your letter and then get up, get dressed and come downstairs. If you are not standing next to me in one hour from now, I shall come and fetch you and carry you down in whatever state of undress you might be.' He was smiling, but she knew better than to ignore his words. He strode out whistling like one of the garden boys – not something she was accustomed to hearing.

She opened the letter and read the words. She perused it twice more to make sure she had not been mistaken. Her brother was right to call her a goose – a simpleton would be more accurate.

She rang the bell and the girl was beside her in a trice.

'We have less than an hour for me to complete my ablutions, do my hair, and for me to be with the duke. Do you think you can do it?'

In fact, she was ready in half the time and was able to devour the toast and weak tea that had been brought up to her. She tied the ribbons on her new bonnet under her chin, checked her pelisse was unwrinkled, pulled on her gloves and was ready to go. As she was dashing downstairs it occurred to her that her cousin had not been to visit. No doubt her brother would explain where she was.

He was standing by the open front door looking every inch the duke, from his coat from Weston's that emphasised his broad shoulders, to his highly polished Hessians.

'You look better, sweetheart. Your eyes are sparkling and your cheeks have colour. I take it the missive from your husband explained to your satisfaction why he isn't here.'

'I wish the silly girl who is looking after me had given me that before she told me he had gone – Jenny would never have made such an error. Now, why had I to come down? What is it you wish to show me?'

He took her arm and all but whisked her across the hall to the front steps. She was speechless when she saw what was waiting for them.

'A chaise – and those chestnuts are new as well. Are they mine? This is your wedding and anniversary present to me?'

'It is indeed. Are you pleased with it?'

She flung her arms around his neck and kissed him on the cheek. 'I understand now why Rushton was so cryptic in his letter. He did not wish to spoil the surprise. I have always wanted my own carriage and team and now I have them. Are you prepared to be driven by me or do you insist on taking the reins?'

'You may drive, as long as you remain in the park. If you wish to go elsewhere then I will take over as I'm not sure you are sufficiently experienced to manage if we met another vehicle in the narrow lanes.'

He was correct as she had never driven on public highways. This was one thing she would insist that her husband taught her so she could take herself to visit neighbours and the local emporiums under her own volition.

Once she was settled on the box she released the brake, took the whip in one hand and the reins in the other. She flicked it expertly above the heads of her team and they moved forward smoothly. Beau was relaxed beside her, obviously not concerned that she would tip them both into a ditch.

She concentrated on her driving for the first mile and then felt confident enough to begin a conversation. 'Where is Beth? I expected to see her this morning.'

'She had arranged to spend the day with Madeline but was prepared to cancel it. I told her to go. We had expected you to have departed by now. She will be returning today so we can dine together.'

'It will be strange for her being in this huge house with just you for company.'

'We have spoken of this, and she has asked my permission to return to her familial home. It would seem that her mother is in indifferent health and would like her daughter to reside with her again.'

'I take it you agreed.'

'I did, of course, with certain provisos. I'm sending Carstairs to take over the management of the estate as it in fact belongs to Beth, not to her adoptive mother. It is my duty to see her inheritance is in the best possible shape so when she marries, her husband will have nothing to complain of.' He smiled and continued. 'He will keep an eye on things and let me know if she gets out of line.'

'The last time we spoke of it, she was determined to wait until she reaches her majority so she can marry her young lieutenant.'

'I told her that if she is still of the same mind this time next year then she has my permission to marry him. I believe her feelings to be sincere – it remains to be seen if Sullivan is as steadfast.'

They bowled along in silence for a while and then an ominous rumble of thunder in the distance made her decide to turn the carriage as soon as she might and return before they got a drenching.

She halted the team neatly, applied the brake, tied the reins around the post and was ready to be handed down from the box. 'That was most enjoyable. Thank you so much. I am a little worried about travelling so far in what is ostensibly an open carriage. Especially as we will not have luggage with us.'

He landed beside her and took her arm affectionately. 'Rushton has that in hand, sweetheart. There's room for a small trunk each on the back and as you are a married couple there can be no objection to you staying overnight if necessary.'

Her skin prickled at his words. She wasn't sure if it was excitement or apprehension at the thought that she might be obliged to share a bedchamber with her husband so soon.

* * *

Rushton got Estelle and Eloise settled in, explained to the governess his requirements, and was then ready to return to collect his bride. He was travelling post-chaise, which was exorbitantly expensive but essential if they were not to have a spare horse or carriage at Silchester again.

He had some overnight necessities already packed and waiting for him when he arrived in Hertfordshire. They would not travel for more than a few hours before stopping for the night at the best posting inn on the route. They would then complete the journey the following day and should be at Castlemere mid-afternoon.

When he reached his destination, the skies were black, and a heavy downpour was imminent. He must be grateful, he supposed, that he had arrived before the rain, but he was now worried Giselle would get soaked and this could not be good for her after being so unwell.

A vigilant footman must have seen the chaise arrive as the front door opened when he reached the top step. He was bowed in and told that his wife and the duke were in the small drawing room, and that refreshments would be served directly.

This house was familiar to him and he had no need to be escorted. The doors were open and his approach must have been heard as his wife arrived to meet him. She flew towards him and he had no option but to open his arms and embrace her.

'You are here a day earlier than we expected. I am so glad to see you as I have missed you dreadfully. Thank you for your birthday gift and I must apologise...'

'No, sweetheart, you must not. It was an unfortunate misunderstanding and entirely my fault. We will say no more about it and start afresh today.'

She tilted her face and he obliged with a kiss. He had intended it to be no more than a gentle touch of his lips on hers but whatever his head said, his body had other ideas. He lifted her from her feet, crushing her softness against his chest and plundered her mouth. Fortunately, Silchester reminded them he was present by clearing his throat loudly.

He slid her down his length and winked at her. 'I have missed you too, my love, but I think we must behave ourselves until we are alone.' His embarrassment would be plain to see and he had no wish to walk into the drawing room as he was.

'Forgive me, I must remove the grime from my travels before I join you. I shall not be above ten minutes.'

He was striding down the corridor with his back to her before she could comment. He kept his coat-tails flipped forward as he bounded up the stairs and into the apartment he was always allocated when he visited here. He dipped his head into a basin of cold water and it did the trick. His stock was a trifle soggy but that couldn't be helped.

Silchester had thoughtfully loaned him garments to change into to dine. He had hoped to eat with Giselle in her sitting room so had not thought these items would be necessary. His host was making it quite clear that he was to remain in his own bed tonight.

They had the rest of their lives to spend together, so waiting another night or two to make love to his wife was a mere bagatelle.

His wife was unaware of his reason for making such a rapid exit but his friend raised an eyebrow and smirked – if you would say that a duke actually did something so mundane.

When they went up to change for dinner he and Giselle walked together. 'I have so much to tell you about my cousin, but it will have to wait until we are in the carriage tomorrow. Shall we still leave if it is raining as it is at the moment?'

'Summer showers, my love – they will pass and it will be sunny and warm tomorrow. There will be little shelter under the hood of the chaise so I hope you have something warm to put on if necessary?'

'I have, and a plain bonnet with no decoration as I had an unfortunate experience with a bunch of cherries when caught in a shower last year.'

'Did you indeed? What happened? I am all agog.'

'The colour ran when they were wet and it looked as if I'd

been in a bloodbath. Which reminds me, my dear, I see you have had your stitches removed and the scar is hardly noticeable.'

He ran his finger along the faint pink line and nodded. 'The physician did a good job. I'm hoping there will not be a similar occurrence in the future. You give me your word you will not throw a book at me next time I upset you?'

Her laughter was infectious. 'I promise; what I cannot do is promise I will not throw a different object.' She released her hold on his arm and dodged into her bedchamber before he could respond to her sally.

He was still smiling as he reached his apartment and was pleased, but not surprised, to find he had a substitute for Penrose ready to dress him for dinner.

14

Giselle took extra time over her appearance as she wished to look her best for her husband. She was wearing a leaf green gown, which would set off the emerald necklace perfectly. Her hair had been arranged in an elaborate style and emerald green glass beads threaded through it on a ribbon.

'There, my lady, you are ready. You look like a princess in that gown.'

She should reprimand the girl for making personal remarks but didn't have the heart as the words were well meant. 'I shall not require you to wait for me this evening, but I will want you here at five tomorrow morning as Lord Rushton and I intend to depart early.'

The girl curtsied and thanked her for giving her the evening free. Giselle was hoping that Rushton would come to her that night as the anticipation of what might be going to happen was making her queasy. What took place between a man and wife, according to her sister, was nothing to fear, but something to look forward to. She prayed that would be the case for her.

He would come to her tonight and she would be ready. It

was going to be easier to receive him in her bedchamber as this time she would already be in the bed in her nightgown and not have to worry about how much clothing she was supposed to remove herself. Madeline had said that she and Grey had no clothes on at all when the act took place. She wasn't sure if she was quite ready for that.

A knock on the door made her heart skip and she thought it might be him coming to collect her. It wasn't – it was her cousin.

'You look divine, Giselle. You should wear deep colours more often. Is that the necklace Rushton gave you?'

'It is – do you like it? I believe it is quite the most beautiful thing I have ever been given.'

Her cousin giggled. 'I should think so too, unless you have a raft of secret admirers plying you with expensive gifts.'

'You are quite outrageous, dearest, and I shall miss you when I go tomorrow. Will you come and stay with us in the autumn or do you think your parent will be too unwell to leave?'

'I shall definitely come, and look forward to it. I suppose Cousin Beau has told you he has given his permission for me to become engaged to my beloved Theodore next year.'

'He has, and I am delighted for you.'

'I am to go and stay with Lady Augusta in a few weeks and then I'm hopeful that I can travel to the Peninsula next spring so my dearest Theodore and I can be married out there.'

'Has my brother given you permission to go abroad?'

'No, I have not mentioned it to him yet and I beg you not to do so until I have my arrangements in place.'

'It shall be our secret, Beth. As long as you give me your word you will not set off unchaperoned and alone.'

'I am not a complete widgeon. I shall only go if I can travel with other ladies.'

They had now reached the gallery and further discussion of

this topic was no longer sensible. Giselle picked up her skirt and began the long descent down the imposing staircase.

She was met at the bottom by her husband. There was no need for him to say anything as his expression said it all. He held out his hand and she took it, revelling in the strength of his gloveless fingers.

'You are *ravissante*. I am the luckiest man in the country to have you as my bride.' His eyes were dark, his cheeks hectic.

'And I am the luckiest young lady to have you as my husband.' She hoped that her smile conveyed her feelings as she could not find the words to express her love.

Beth coughed politely and they sprang apart. 'I'm sorry to disturb your romantic moment, but I cannot stand about on the stairs all night.'

His rich deep laughter filled the hall and made her feel quite flustered. He pulled her arm through his and they strolled in perfect harmony into the drawing room where Beau was awaiting them.

After a delicious dinner, the four of them played cards until the tea tray came in. Then Rushton reminded her they were to leave at dawn, so she bid the company goodnight and retired to her bedchamber. He would come to her tonight, and she glowed all over at the thought of it.

She lay awake listening to every sound but he did not visit and eventually she fell asleep, not sure if she was disappointed or relieved.

The temporary maid appeared at the appointed hour and Giselle was dressed and ready to depart in good time. She was surprised and touched that both her brother and her cousin had got up to bid her farewell.

* * *

The weather remained fine and warm and they were able to complete the journey from Hertfordshire to Essex without mishap. They had stayed overnight in a fine inn in an apartment with two bedchambers and a dressing room.

They had been travelling for three hours the following day when he drew the chestnuts to a halt. 'From here, my love, we are travelling on my land.'

'Do you have many acres?'

'Around two thousand, a village, two hamlets and a dozen or more farms – I forget exactly how many.'

'I had no idea you were such a substantial landowner. At what distance from us is your nearest acquaintance?'

He frowned. 'I misremember exactly. I have not entertained since my first wife died and she dealt with that sort of thing. My butler, Frobisher, will no doubt have a list he can supply us with. Are you happy to have a garden party and ball as soon as it can be arranged?'

'I assume that your housekeeper will be able to take care of things. What is her name – I wish to be able to address her correctly when we arrive?'

'Johnson – they have both been with the family since I was a boy. Perhaps it is time for them to retire and for you to find your own staff.'

'I certainly don't intend to do so in the foreseeable future, my dear. I will need their guidance until I understand how you like your home to be run.'

'Would you like to take the reins the last few miles? It is rare indeed to meet another vehicle on this lane as it only leads to Castlemere.'

He carefully climbed across her and she took his place. It took a further hour before she saw her future home in the distance. Although aware she was going to be residing in a building that resembled a castle she had no idea it was an actual castle built on a hill so it dominated the landscape.

She drove the chaise through an imposing gateway and then along a further half a mile of drive then saw the carriage would have to cross a bridge over the moat. She wasn't sure she was sufficiently skilled with the reins to do that without mishap.

'I think you should drive the remaining distance, Rushton. I should hate to run us into the moat.'

'I shall do no such thing; you are quite capable of negotiating the bridge. Bring the team to a slow walk and they will do the rest for you.'

His assumption was correct and although her heart was in her mouth as the wheels echoed on the bridge, at no time did she think they were in any danger.

'To the right, the turning circle and the entrance that we use is at the rear of the castle.'

She scarcely had time to pull on the brake and tie the reins around the post before their daughters raced down the steps squealing with excitement. Miss Gibbons made no attempt to stop them but remained in the doorway smiling.

Her husband was down and at her side before she had begun to climb out. He reached up and lifted her as if she weighed nothing at all and placed her on her feet so she could receive the children in her arms.

'Mama, Papa, you are here at last. We have missed you dreadfully. Mama, are you quite well now? Can we show you all the things that our papa has done for you at Castlemere?' Estelle tugged at her hand.

'I am fully restored, thank you, sweetheart. Now, if you take this hand and your sister takes the other, you can lead me in.'

It took over an hour to see her new home and she was delighted with everything she saw. 'I had thought there would only be stone walls and shields and armour everywhere. I own I am relieved that the ancient part of this building is not commonly used.'

'My grandfather had this modern addition built on the rear of the castle whilst preserving the old. I am glad it meets with your approval. It has cost a prodigious amount of money and I should have been most displeased if you had not.'

She stiffened for a second and then saw his eyes twinkling. 'You are teasing me, sir, and I do not like it one bit. I was brought up to think that to mention money is unacceptable in polite circles.' She tossed her head and sniffed loudly and he laughed out loud.

'There is a cold collation waiting on the terrace and the girls are to join us as today is a special occasion. Do you wish to change your raiment first or are you happy to proceed?'

'I took the opportunity to wash my face and hands and remove my bonnet, as you can see, when I was in my apartment. I see no necessity for changing one's clothes every five minutes; twice a day is more than enough as far as I'm concerned.'

'Then we are in agreement on one thing at least. You will discover that I dress informally when here, and I don't expect you to change for dinner unless you wish to – I certainly don't.'

'Then I shall follow your lead on this, my dear. I shall only put on an evening gown when we are entertaining or going out.' She stopped and looked sharply at him. 'You do go out sometimes to visit your neighbours for a dinner, rout or soirée?'

'I certainly intend to do so now I have remarried. The ball and a garden party will serve to re-establish my connection with the neighbourhood. I'm certain we will be invited to any number of parties, and dinners and so on once it is known I have a beautiful bride to introduce.'

Giselle was content with his answer and they walked arm in

arm to the terrace. From here she could see the gardens, the expanse of lawn kept neatly manicured by a flock of sheep, and the ornamental lake. Her gasp as she saw the fountain made the expense of having it repaired worthwhile.

She ran to the edge of the balustrade and the girls joined her. 'Do you like it, Mama? It was only switched on this morning in honour of your arrival.'

'I do, Eloise. It is quite beautiful the way the sunlight makes rainbows in the water. Is that a maze I see to the left?'

'It is. We like to play in that. We shall show you how to find your way in and out without getting lost—'

'Not today, Estelle – that can wait until tomorrow. Now, what would you like me to fetch you from the fine selection we have waiting for us?'

It was the custom for the gentleman to serve the ladies if there were no footmen present – and there weren't – so she led the girls to the table and all three of them sat.

'Do you have a hothouse here and grow your own oranges and lemons?' she asked Rushton.

'We do and we also have pineapples, peaches and grapes. I shall show you around the gardens on another day.'

'There is no urgency. I am quite content to take my time examining my new home.'

'What would you like?' He looked under the silver lids, which had been placed over each plate of food to keep them from the flies and other insects that might decide to investigate. 'There is a selection of cold cuts, salads, chutneys, game pie and also a blancmange, a fruit pie of some sort and a jug of cream.'

'What would you like, girls? I intend to have a little of everything.' They agreed they would follow her lead and she settled them at the table, making sure they had a napkin spread across their laps.

A while later they were replete. 'Look, children, Miss Gibbons has come to collect you. Run along now. I shall come and see you before you retire.'

Obediently they scrambled off their chairs curtsied to her and their father and scampered off. He watched them go, his eyes alight with love. 'The governess Carstairs appointed has been a godsend. My daughters are happier than they have ever been before.'

His words were like a deluge of icy water over her head. She had thought it was her arrival in their lives that had changed them, but he obviously considered Miss Gibbons the reason for their happiness. Did he also consider her an inadequate parent, too young and inexperienced to take over the reins of the household?

'I intend to speak to Johnson this afternoon. What time do we dine? I shall make sure our meeting does not overrun as we have a lot to discuss.'

He stretched across the table and patted her hand. 'We dine at six o'clock – I do not like to keep country hours. There is no necessity for you to speak to Johnson. She has been running this establishment since Charlotte died and will do everything that is required. You have no need to worry yourself about anything, sweetheart.'

She swallowed the lump in her throat and looked away so he wouldn't see her tears. 'Excuse me, Rushton, I am fatigued after our drive and shall retire to my apartment to rest for the remainder of the afternoon. I shall be down in good time this evening.'

Not waiting for him to stand and pull back her chair, she was on her feet and walking briskly towards the French doors before he had time to react. Fortunately, her memory was good and she was able to find her chambers with no difficulty.

The first thing she did was bolt the door that connected to his room. She would push a chair under the handle of her sitting room before she retired that night. If her husband didn't consider her mature enough to run his house or be a parent to his daughters, then as far as she was concerned she wasn't old enough to become his true wife. Until he treated her with the respect she deserved their union would remain unconsummated.

Jenny was unusually subdued but Giselle couldn't summon the energy to question her as to the reason why she was not her usual effervescent self. 'Lord Rushton does not require me to put on an evening gown when we are dining informally at home. Therefore, one of the sprig muslins will suffice. As I now have my own bathing room arrange for hot water to be brought up at four o'clock.'

'Yes, my lady. Will that be all?'

'Thank you, it will. Spend the afternoon getting to know your new surroundings and the other servants working here.'

Once she was alone she wandered into this newfangled bath that was long enough for her to stretch out her legs and not sit with them under her chin, or dangle them over the edge, as she had in the hip bath. She looked with interest at the aperture at the narrow end through which the water would vanish when she was done. There was a neat plug to close this hole so the water would remain in place until it was finished with.

Knowing that the servants would no longer be obliged to carry buckets of dirty water back down the narrow staircase would make her enjoy the pleasure of immersing herself in scented water even more. It was a shame they would still have to carry it up the stairs – but she was sure they would be happy that they had half the work in future.

Unlike some of her peers, who rarely bathed and thought

An Accommodating Husband

that concealing their odour with perfume was sufficient, she liked to bathe at least once a month – now she thought she would indulge in this pleasurable pastime every week.

As she was relaxing on the soft feather pillows in her newly refurbished bed, it occurred to her that as this was the only bathing room installed, her husband might demand to share its use.

15

Rushton spoke to Frobisher and Johnson about the forthcoming events to be held at Castlemere and they were delighted he was going to start entertaining again.

'I don't wish Lady Giselle to be bothered with any of the preparations. By rights we should be on our wedding trip where she would have no responsibilities or onerous decisions to make. Do I make myself clear?'

The butler bowed and the housekeeper curtsied. There was no need to talk further as they understood exactly what he required of them. His estate manager had business matters to discuss pertaining to the numerous farms and so he was closeted in his study for the remainder of the afternoon.

Although he did not change into evening rig he always freshened up and put on a crisp, starched neckcloth. He had heard movement next door so Giselle must be getting ready as well. He raised his hand to knock on the communicating door then thought better of it. Time enough to make his first visit to her rooms tonight.

His pulse quickened and he could not prevent his mouth

curving. This marriage was not of his choosing, but the more time he spent with his bride the better he liked her and the happier he was about the enforced arrangement.

As the *al fresco* luncheon had been so successful he had asked for dinner to be served on the terrace as well. He was not a romantic man but he rather thought he would enjoy seeing the sun set over the lake in the company of his beautiful young wife.

Frobisher had been told not to serve alcohol to her – he would have claret with his meal and cognac afterwards as usual. He didn't want a repeat of what had occurred at his wedding breakfast.

'Good evening, I'm sorry if I have kept you waiting, Rushton, but I was spending time with the girls before I came down.'

He gripped the balustrade and took a steadying breath. He had not heard her approach and she had taken him unawares so he had almost risen from the ground at her words.

Slowly he turned. She had changed out of her travelling gown but into something no more than pretty. He had thought she would make more effort to please him as this was to be her true wedding night.

'I have arranged for us to dine out here whilst the weather is so fine. Today is like a perfect summer's evening. I have heard cuckoos, and the swallows are plentiful – if we are lucky we might still be able to hear nightingales in the woods when it gets dark.'

She did not seem particularly impressed by his remark. In fact, she was withdrawn and her customary smile absent. Something had upset her and he was determined to discover what it was so that he could put matters right. He wanted her to be happy and he was going to do his damnedest to make sure that happened.

'There will be three removes only with each course as we had such a substantial repast earlier.'

'I was tempted to send word that I didn't require dinner at all but thought that might be misconstrued by both yourself and your staff. I'm not accustomed to eating so much in the middle of the day and have little appetite for dinner.'

A footman glided up and offered her a choice of orgeat, ratafia or lemonade. She pursed her lips and stared pointedly at his glass of sherry. She shook her head and the servant disappeared. This was not going well and he had no notion what had caused her to change towards him.

He was unused to dealing with young ladies and had not spent time alone with one since he had married his beloved Charlotte when he was the same age as his present wife. The evening lurched from one stilted comment to another and neither of them did justice to the splendid repast that had been served to them. Cook would be disappointed after she had put in so much effort on their behalf.

When the final plates were removed, she put down her napkin. 'I hope you will excuse me, sir, but I intend to retire. I am still not fully recovered from my megrim.' She stood up and nodded politely. 'I bid you goodnight. I shall see you at breakfast.'

He stood, as was expected of him, but his hands were clenched. She could not have made it plainer. She was his wife and he was not going to be gainsaid on this matter. She had no wish for him to visit her tonight. He allowed her to reach the French doors before he answered.

'You will see me before that. I shall be joining you shortly.'

Her back was turned to him but he saw her stiffen. She made no response but continued on her journey and he wished the words unsaid. With a snarl of frustration he swept the glasses and cutlery from the table, and the resulting noise brought the butler to investigate.

He didn't stay to explain. What he did in his own house was his business and it wasn't for his staff to question his actions; it was their job to follow his instructions and clear up his mess. He vaulted over the stone balustrade and landed amongst the thorns of the rose bushes growing below. It took him several minutes to extricate himself and this did nothing for his temper.

What he needed was a gallop around the park, jumping as many hedges and ditches as he could find until his fury dissipated and he was calm enough to return. Eventually he returned his lathered mount to the stables with a curt apology to the groom who would have to walk the horse for an hour to cool him down.

He was in little better case himself and would need to do something about it before he went to her. On his ride he had understood why she was so reserved. She was nervous about what would happen between them and this had caused her to behave so out of character. It had been different when he had first made love to Charlotte – they were both inexperienced in the bedroom arts and learned to enjoy each other's bodies together.

Giselle's initiation would be gentle and loving, and he would cause her as little hurt as possible. If they could not share pleasure in this way then their future looked bleak indeed.

* * *

'I shall not need you again tonight, Jenny, so you may have the remainder of the evening free. I shall ring when I want you in the morning. Could you please put out my riding habit, boots, hat, gloves and whip so I can go out at dawn without disturbing you?'

The girl curtsied but didn't reply – if she wasn't so on edge herself Giselle would have sat her maid down and discovered what was bothering her.

The windows of her bedchamber overlooked the woods and she could indeed hear nightingales singing. Usually this would lift her spirits but tonight they failed to do so. No sooner had Jenny gone than she set about blockading herself into her bedroom. The communicating door had a chairback under the handle and she defied anyone, even someone as strong as Rushton, to open it. The door into her sitting room had a bolt, which she had pushed across. The only way anyone could get into her room was via the servants' entrance.

She frowned as she swung the door back and forth. It was all very well being certain she would not be disturbed when she had been at Silchester Court, but she had no idea if Rushton would be familiar with the passages and staircases that his servants used.

Surely a gentleman would not intrude when he was so obviously not wanted? Eventually she would have to allow him into her bed, but not at the moment, not when she was so angry with him treating her like one of his daughters. The deliberate omission of alcohol at dinner had only added to her resentment. She was not a simpleton – she would not have taken more than half a glass of claret. However, she was an adult and should have been given the choice, not have had it made for her.

After patrolling the bedchamber for an hour she came to a decision. She would remain dressed and sit in a chair in the far corner of the room where she could not be seen if he did venture through the dressing room to reach her.

Her husband was not the sort of man who would force his

attentions on any woman. If he could not seduce her into his bed he would leave her be – at least for the moment. He was entitled to go anywhere in the house he pleased, so by rights she should have left the doors open. Finding his passage blocked would only make him more determined to get in.

She would open the doors and rely on his honour to keep her safe tonight. Then the handle turned on the communicating door. She was too late. He was here and she didn't have the courage to remove the obstacle when he was rattling at the door so insistently.

'Giselle, I wish to come in. You will remove whatever is blocking the door immediately.'

If he had been more conciliatory, had apologised, had asked her in a loving manner, she would have done as he requested without hesitation. Instead she shrank back into her seat and prayed he would give up; she doubted she could reason with him when he was so angry.

The door rattling ceased and she thought she was safe. Then he put his shoulder to the door from her sitting room and the bolt held. This time he didn't demand to be let in but she could imagine his teeth were grinding and his eyes were hard.

She heard the outer door close. He would not be denied. He would certainly find his way through the dressing room and she would suffer for her disobedience. Thanking the good Lord above that she had remained fully clothed, she ran to the door that led into her sitting room, unbolted it, and fled through into the passageway. There was little point in going downstairs as all the doors would be locked – possibly with a key that only the housekeeper and butler would have.

No – she would go to the attics and hide herself there. She had not stopped to light a candle and by the time she had made her way up the second flight of narrow stairs she bitterly regretted this omission. The only way she could move forward was by running her fingers along the limewashed walls and shuffling forward until her toes touched the next step.

Perspiration was prickling between her shoulder blades by the time she reached the door. She found the latch and lifted it and was relieved that moonlight filtered in through the small windowpanes and she was able to find her way without breaking her neck on the pieces of furniture, trunks and other oddments that had been stored up there.

She rummaged around until she found a trunk in which were stored what looked like old flags. She removed several, two to spread out and sit on and another to wrap around herself as it was much colder than she had anticipated.

After a miserable few hours the first birds began their dawn chorus and she thought it would be safe to return to her apartment. With the attic door propped open she was able to negotiate the stairs without difficulty and then creep through the house and into her own rooms.

The overmantel clock struck four as she passed. This would allow her to get a few hours' rest before being obliged to get up. The early morning ride would have to wait until tomorrow. She stepped into her bedchamber and her bladder almost emptied when her husband spoke from his position sprawled on her bed.

'There you are, my love. I hope that you enjoyed your sojourn in the attics.'

Only by clutching the doorpost did she remain upright. She was unable to speak and thought for an awful moment she was going to cast up her accounts in front of him. Then, despite her best efforts, her legs gave way beneath her and she slid slowly to the floor.

The bed creaked, his stockinged feet thudded to the floor

and he was on his knees beside her. 'I am a brute to frighten you like that. Put your arm around my neck and I will carry you.'

She was incapable of even doing this simple thing. Her face was wet and she let the tears fall. He had outwitted her and she must suffer whatever punishment he had in store.

* * *

With his precious burden in his arms Rushton regained his feet in one smooth movement. He had followed her wild flight last night and watched from the shadows until she was comfortable and he was sure she would come to no harm. Then he had returned to wait for her, ashamed that his anger had frightened her so badly she had felt the need to hide from him.

He didn't take her to her bed but into her sitting room where she would feel safe. He sat on the *chaise longue*, swung his legs up and then settled her comfortably against his chest, all the while stroking her back and murmuring soothing words of encouragement.

'Don't cry. I cannot bear to see you so distraught. Did you really think I would ravish you? Demand my conjugal rights when you are so obviously reluctant?'

Her whispered reply was incoherent and she clutched his waistcoat and burrowed her head into his shoulder. Her tears became sobs and he rocked her as he would have done one of his daughters until she was done.

Carefully he removed one hand and untied his neckcloth – that would have to do as a handkerchief for now. 'Here, little one, dry your eyes and blow your nose and then we must talk.'

She did as he instructed. He was about to lift her from his lap but she had relaxed in his arms and he didn't have the heart to insist she move. It was going to be difficult having this conversation when every inch of her was pressed against his length, reminding him just how desirable she was.

'Giselle, you must give me your word that you will never lock me out of your rooms again. And I vow that I will not make love to you until you are ready.'

'Then I promise I will not do it again. It was decidedly cold in the attics and I have no wish to spend further time up there.'

He shook her gently. 'It serves you right for running away from me. I am sad that you thought so little of me. We have the rest of our lives to get to know each other and I am content to wait until you are sufficiently grown-up to become my true wife and take control of my household and daughters. Until then you will not be burdened...'

As he had been speaking she had become still, her body tense, but he was still taken by surprise when she tore herself from his arms and scrambled to her feet.

'You do not know me at all, Rushton. Why do you think I was so incensed that I did not wish to share my bed with you? I am not afraid of what happens between a man and his wife – indeed, with any other gentleman I would be eagerly looking forward to the experience.

'As the marriage remains unconsummated, as far as I'm concerned it is null and void. I intend to leave here and reside in Northumbria. And you, my lord, may go to perdition.'

Her hair was in disarray, her gown mired with cobwebs, her face tear-streaked – she had never looked more beautiful. He must tread carefully if he was not to lose her forever. He stood up and walked slowly towards her, keeping his movements unthreatening and his expression bland.

'I beg you, Giselle, do not do anything precipitate. This is a large house and there is no need for us to meet at all if that's what you wish. Please remain here for a few weeks and then, if you still wish to leave, I shall not prevent you.'

She stared at him through narrowed eyes and he thought she was going to refuse. Then she nodded. 'I shall do so, but for the girls, not for you. My eyes are open to the truth of the situation. You are right to call me naïve; I believed your lies when you said that you loved me. I know that you do not; you were just doing the honourable thing.

'I cannot turn my feelings off so easily – but I'm sure with time I shall succeed. I'm sorry that you will never be free to marry again and produce an heir – but you have only yourself to blame for the situation.'

'Thank you.' He walked away from her, finally understanding what she meant to him now it was too late.

16

Rushton kept to his word and Giselle spent the next week without being obliged to spend more than a few brief moments in his company. At no time did he try and engage her in long conversations or persuade her to change her mind about leaving. He was unfailingly polite, charming, treated her with the utmost respect, but not as if she was his wife.

The staff responded to her requests with alacrity but did not treat her as if she was indeed mistress of the house – more like an honoured guest. The only ones who made her feel as if she was indeed no longer Lady Giselle Sheldon but Lady Giselle Rushton were Eloise and Estelle.

They spent the morning doing their schoolwork and the afternoons with her. She had discovered they were both excellent riders and each had their own pony so she took them out for a gentle hack most days and for a drive in her new carriage on the others.

She had no idea when the ball or the garden party was to be held. No one had informed her, let alone consulted her wishes. The house had been cleaned from top to bottom, carpets taken up and beaten, the curtains shaken and dusted, the windows cleaned with vinegar and paper. One would have thought this would have been done during the redecoration and refurbishment.

A week after her confrontation with Rushton she saw that the ballroom was being decorated with elaborate vases of flowers. This was the outside of enough – until she left Castlemere she was the lady of the house and it was her right to know what was going on and to have some input into the arrangements.

The fact that she did not intend to remain here was between herself and her husband – as far as they were concerned everything was as it should be.

She went to the bell strap and pulled it hard. When a footman arrived she sent him to fetch the housekeeper. She stood, tapping her foot, awaiting the arrival of this woman to whom she had yet to speak in person.

Johnson appeared at the open door and curtsied. 'You wish to see me, my lady?'

'I am most displeased with you. I am the mistress here. Why have you not brought the menus, accounts and other information to me each morning as you should?' She fixed the woman with her fiercest stare.

Instead of being upset or countered by this interrogation the woman smirked. 'I beg your pardon, my lady, but the master said you were not to be bothered with household arrangements. That he wished you to...'

'Lord Rushton is not in charge of domestic matters, Johnson; I am. You have been remiss in your duties and unless you wish to be dismissed without reference you will in future do as you ought. Do I make myself quite clear?'

The woman flinched and her superior smile vanished. She curtsied, more deeply this time. 'I understand exactly, my lady. If you would excuse me for a few moments I will fetch everything I should have shown you when you arrived last week.'

The housekeeper scurried off in a swirl of navy bombazine. The drawing room was not the correct place for her to discuss domestic matters but she had no notion where she should go. Her own sitting room upstairs was equally unsuitable and she could hardly use Rushton's study.

She rang the bell again and this time Frobisher appeared. He too looked decidedly uncomfortable. He bowed deeply. 'Yes, my lady, how can I be of service?'

'Conduct me to the chamber the previous Lady Rushton used as her study. Then have Johnson find me there.'

He conducted her to a part of the house she had not visited before. Why had the children not brought her here when they had taken her around? The furniture in the pretty room was shrouded in holland covers but the butler whisked them off as if such a task was normal for him.

She waved him away and he vanished with the cloths under his arm. There was a sofa and two matching chintz-covered chairs, a pretty table, behind which stood a chair – another faced this. This was obviously used as the desk as there were the necessary accoutrements upon its highly polished surface.

The room had not been used for several years but was surprisingly well maintained – no dust on the surfaces and everything shining with beeswax.

The housekeeper came in, her arms full of ledgers and papers, and immediately placed her burden on the table. She waited politely for Giselle to take her place and then sat opposite on the other chair.

'This is the invitation list for the ball, my lady; this for the garden party. I am pleased to tell you that we have had no refusals – everyone has accepted.'

Giselle glanced down the columns of names, doing a rapid mental calculation. It would seem that there would be more than one hundred coming to the formal event. 'Exactly when is this ball to take place?'

Her question startled the housekeeper. Her cheeks coloured and she fiddled with the ledger. 'It is to be held at the end of July, my lady, two weeks from today. The garden party will be on the following Saturday. You will see from the list that this event is for the villagers, his lordship's tenants and their families.'

'Where is the list of entertainment to be provided for the children? I take it there will be a Punch and Judy, stilt-walkers, fire-eaters and a tug of war?'

'There is no list, ma'am; we were not instructed to arrange for any specific entertainment. Just to provide refreshments and allow visitors to wander around the park.'

'Good grief! That is not what I call a garden party. There must be music so in the evening folk can dance if they wish – the coach house could be used for that. Are there any Romanies in the vicinity at the moment?'

'There are, my lady. His lordship allows them to stay on the far side of the woods where there is fresh water and plenty of firewood.'

'Then someone must go down to their encampment. No – I shall go myself as I know exactly what I want from them.' The housekeeper was about to comment but thought better of it. 'If I had been consulted last week things would be already in hand. There must be two rooms put aside for the ladies, one for the gentlemen, with the necessary facilities.

'I want lanterns on the terrace and hanging from the trees so the guests can walk on the lawn if they so wish. I take it you have sufficient card tables and fresh packs of cards? It is possible some of the gentlemen will wish to play billiards, so that room must also be made available.'

Johnson had been busily scribbling on her notepad, feverishly dipping her pen in the inkwell and scattering blots all over the page in her effort to keep up. 'I have that all down, my lady. It is so long since there was any entertaining here that we are sadly out of practice. Everything will be as you wish on the night, and I apologise—'

'There is no need to do that. As long as you ensure everything is as I want it to be for both events then you and I will work well together. Has Frobisher taken on any extra staff or will the outside men be used as extra footmen at the ball?'

'I have taken on a dozen extra girls from the village and Mr Frobisher has done the same for the men that he will need. We keep spare livery and gowns so I dare say no one will notice the difference.'

'That will be all, Johnson. Ensure I see the menus every morning in future. Leave the accounts books here.'

After flicking though the figures Giselle was satisfied everything was in order. After her older sister, Madeline, had left to marry Lord Carshalton it had been her task to oversee the household. Although, like here, the staff were of long standing and everything ran smoothly without the intervention of herself or Beau.

Her eyes filled as she thought of how happy her sister and brothers were in their own marriages. All were love matches – as she had thought hers was. Obtaining an annulment required an Act of Parliament and would bring scandal down on both families. Even as she had threatened this, she'd known it would be nigh on impossible.

This marriage had been the most dreadful mistake. She should have kept to her original plan to retire to the wilds of

Northumbria until the gossip settled. Then neither she nor Rushton would be trapped in a loveless union.

She dried her eyes on her sleeve, something she'd not done since leaving the schoolroom. Her summation of the facts was not accurate as whatever his feelings, she was still hopelessly in love with him.

A movement outside caught her attention. Rushton was striding across the grass, deep in conversation with the head gardener. He should be occupied for the remainder of the morning so she would take her chaise and drive to the Romany camp before he got wind of what she proposed. Visiting such a place was not something a young lady should contemplate doing, but she was determined to go. With luck, there would be those she wanted to entertain the children amongst their number. The travelling people who stopped on Sheldon land had always been friendly and polite to her when she visited. Why should these be any different?

* * *

Rushton returned to the house mid-afternoon and saw his daughters playing on the swings that had been erected in the trees at the edge of the lawn. Where was Giselle? She was always with them at this time. They were accompanied by two nursemaids so perhaps Miss Gibbons was with his wife.

He lengthened his stride and headed for the house. He was met by the butler in the entrance hall.

'My lord, might I be permitted to have a few words in private?'

'Speak up, man, I wish to find Lady Giselle.'

'It is on this subject I wish to—'

'For God's sake, what is it? Has my wife met with an accident?'

'No, my lord, but she took her carriage and went to the Romany encampment two hours ago and has not yet returned.'

Rushton didn't stop to hear more but set off at a run for the stables. Five minutes later he was galloping towards the woods where the camp was situated. What bee had got into her bonnet to send her here? He had allowed her too much freedom these past days and if anything untoward had happened to her he would never forgive himself.

The Romany camp was not a place for a young lady to visit without the protection of a gentleman – in fact it wasn't a place a young lady should go to at all. What had possessed her to venture there? He allowed them to use the bottom meadow and to take what game they wanted from his woods whilst they were there. This way there was no pilfering from the farms or from the villagers' gardens as they could feed themselves for free from his land.

His horse shortened its stride and sailed over the hedge, landing in the field adjacent to the caravans. He steadied his mount and by the time he exited the field he was travelling at a more decorous pace. There was no sign of the chaise.

'Hey, you there. I am looking for her ladyship. Has she visited here?' The slovenly fellow he had addressed ignored him and slouched away. If this was to be their attitude, then they would not be allowed here again.

'Beggin' your pardon, me lord, her ladyship was here but she left a while ago. You'll have missed her if you come across country.' A handsome woman with a colourful head covering addressed him from the doorway of her caravan.

'Thank you. Why did she come here?'

'She was arrangin' things for the garden party next week, me lord. I told her as you wouldn't be pleased about her comin' on her own.'

Rushton bit back a pithy retort. It was hardly this woman's fault that Giselle had chosen to come unchaperoned and without his permission. He nodded and kicked his horse into a gallop, determined to arrive home before she did. What he had to say to her was best said inside and not in a country lane where they might be overheard by one of his labourers working in the fields.

He erupted from the wood to see her dismounting from the carriage and about to make her way inside. He could hardly yell at her to wait, but once she was through the door she might well retire to her apartment where he could not go. Dammit to hell! He was master here and would go where the hell he pleased.

He vaulted from the saddle and tossed the reins to a lad waiting to receive them. He would not run after her – that would be undignified – but his long strides covered the distance almost as fast and he was no more than a few seconds behind her.

'Lady Giselle, a moment of your time if you please.' His voice carried wonderfully across the hall, causing her to stumble as she was about to ascend the stairs.

She turned and smiled brightly at him. He was not fooled for a moment. She was as angry as he, but like him would not reveal her feelings in front of the staff.

'My lord, forgive me but I have been out in an open carriage and need to repair the damage to my appearance before I can accommodate your wishes. If you would care to wait in the library I will join you as soon I can.' This was spoken crisply, but loud enough for a lurking footman to hear.

He gritted his teeth. 'I shall expect you within a quarter of an hour, my lady.' He nodded and she returned the gesture.

She ran lightly up the stairs and he watched her with appreciation. Despite his fury, every time he caught a glimpse of her trim ankle he was reminded how much he desired her. Reluctantly his lips curved. A pungent odour was wafting up to him and he realised he was more in need of fresh raiment than she, as he had been galloping across the countryside like a lunatic.

Having demanded that she return promptly he had better do the same himself. He bounded after her and roared for Penrose as he flung open his bedchamber door. There was no time to change his shirt but with a fresh cravat, polished Hessians and brushed jacket he would do. He had completed his ablutions in record time and was in the library three minutes before the allotted time.

He had barely time to position himself in the centre of the carpet when his wife sailed in. 'You wish to speak to me, Rushton? What is so urgent it could not have waited until we were both recovered from our exertions?'

He pointed to the chair he had placed facing him. She glanced at it but remained where she was. 'What were you thinking to visit that place unescorted?'

She raised an eyebrow, which did not amuse him. 'Good heavens? Is that what all the fuss is about? I thought there had been some catastrophic event that I must be made aware of.' She strolled to the far end of the room and turned her back on him before continuing to speak. 'I do not need your permission...'

His fury, which had been barely under control, erupted and he closed the distance between them and gripped her shoulders, spinning her around to face him. He was about to tell her exactly what he thought of her impertinence, that he was her husband whatever she thought about the matter and would do as she was told, but the words remained unsaid.

He watched as her cheeks turned pale and her lovely eyes

widened in fear. Instantly, he released her but to his horror she swayed and he thought her about to collapse. He reached out to steady her but she recoiled and held her hands in front of her as if expecting him to strike her.

'I am sorry. I did not think. Please excuse me...'

'Sweetheart, do not look so terrified. I would never hurt you. I apologise for my anger. I had no wish to frighten you.'

Her throat convulsed and she turned her back on him a second time. This was no insult but an attempt to regain her equilibrium. Would she cry? Had he reduced her to tears by his rage? Then she spoke, her voice was so soft he could barely discern what she said.

'I often visited with the Romany families when living at Silchester Court. I didn't think that there could be any objection to my doing so or I would have asked your permission.'

'I arrived there after you had left...'

This, for some reason, straightened her shoulders and she turned to face him. 'How could you have done so as there is only one lane to the site? I would have seen you...'

He smiled ruefully. 'I crossed country – in both directions. Which is why I was in more disarray than you when we met in the hall just now.'

'You came after me? Why was that?'

'I feared for your safety, Giselle. If anything happened to you...'

Her expression changed and she extended her hand. 'You were more likely to come to grief than I, but I do appreciate your concern.'

He took her fingers in his and raised them to his lips. He kissed her knuckles, but what he wanted to do was snatch her into his embrace and make love to her until she agreed to remain with him. Her cheeks regained their colour and he saw tears in her eyes.

'Please, my dear, won't you be seated so you may explain to me what prompted your visit to that camp?'

When she had finished telling him her reasons he was delighted that she had decided to take on her role as mistress of the house. He hid his feelings behind an amused smile. 'I had no idea that a garden party must include so much entertainment.'

'That is a Banbury tale, my lord, as you have attended more than one at Silchester and could not have failed to see what takes place. An entertainment should be exactly that – I cannot see walking about the park would be considered a good day out by any of your tenants and villagers.'

He tried to look offended. 'Surely receiving a free meal and ale would be largesse enough?'

'Both of these events are supposed to be celebrating our nuptials so...' Her voice trailed away and she looked down and fiddled with her skirt.

'Giselle, my love, look at me.' He waited until she raised her head. 'I know your feelings on this subject, but I feel quite differently. I am the luckiest man in the country to have married you and if you would let me, I believe I could make you happy too.'

'I have been thinking on this subject. I love your daughters as if they were my own and it would break my heart to abandon them. I wanted to stop loving you, but I have found it impossible to turn off those feelings so easily.'

'Then you are prepared to stay? To give me a chance to show you how much I love you.'

Then she was in his arms and he forgot they were in the library with the door open and likely to be disturbed.

17

Giselle revelled in the touch of his mouth on hers and instinctively pressed closer to him. How could she have doubted his avowals of love? He wouldn't have ridden *ventre à terre* across country, risking a broken neck, if he didn't care for her as much as she did for him. Her doubts and reservations evaporated under the heat of his mouth and she was hot all over.

Then, unexpectedly, he disentangled her hands from the hair at the back of his neck and gently lifted her away. He turned his back before he spoke to her, his voice sounding strangely gruff. 'I think you had better go before I do something we will both regret. Will you dine with me tonight, sweetheart?'

'Of course I will.'

'Then we shall change; wear one of your new evening gowns for me.'

She was about to enquire if he was feeling unwell as he did sound rather strange, but then she recalled something she had been told by Madeline about the changes that happened to a gentleman when they wished to make love to a woman. Flustered beyond belief at this immodest thought, she picked up her skirts and dashed from the room.

If she hadn't heard her daughters coming downstairs from the schoolroom she would have retreated to the privacy of her apartment to mull over what had happened. Instead, she composed her features, fanned her cheeks in the vain hope they would cool down before she met them, and made her way to the entrance hall.

They spent a jolly afternoon playing cricket. Estelle had rounded up four extra team members from the stable yard and the garden. The boys, naturally, were delighted to be playing cricket instead of doing their usual chores.

'Mama, are we really to have as many exciting things at our garden party as you had at Silchester?'

'Yes, Eloise, we are. I particularly wanted to make it similar to the one I missed because I was unwell.'

'Can Miss Gibbons come too?'

'Good heavens, children, you must not ask Lady Giselle such a thing on my behalf.'

'Miss Gibbons will be an honoured guest. She will have the afternoon free from her duties and you will be with your father and I for the afternoon.'

The governess smiled her thanks as the children dashed ahead, eager to get to the nursery where their tea would be awaiting them.

'I know when you were appointed, Miss Gibbons, you were promised every afternoon free. I apologise that this has not always been possible now we are at Castlemere.'

'I did not expect it to be, my lady. I am happier here than I have ever been in my life before. For the first time, I am living in comfort, have delightful children to educate and believe that my modest efforts are appreciated by the family I work for.'

'They certainly are. I'm hoping there will be further children for you to educate in the future so you may remain with us indefinitely.'

Speaking her thoughts out loud made them seem real and not just daydreams. She had already instructed Jenny to put out the most beautiful gown she owned. Tonight, whatever her husband's feelings on the matter, she was determined to become his true bride. If he failed to come to her then she would be brazen and go in to him.

They were dining at seven o'clock – an hour later than usual. This would give her ample time to bathe before she got dressed in her finery. As far as she was aware Rushton had not made use of the bathing room. After tonight she would suggest that he took his turn in this wondrous place whenever he wished to.

The thought that he would be entirely without clothes made her bodice unaccountably tight. She was quite sure she had no wish to see him unclothed, but she could not help wondering what he looked like beneath his skintight unmentionables and shoulder-hugging jackets.

The gown she had selected was in cream silk, the bodice had an inset of dark gold flowers and the puffed sleeves were edged with a similar gold material. The hem had no rouleaux or ribbons but was embroidered with tiny gold beads. On this occasion, she had asked for the underskirt to be cream as well as she thought the beads and insets were enough decoration and colour.

A long, narrow ribbon of plaited dark gold and cream silk was threaded through her hair. Her slippers were made from the same material and complemented her ensemble perfectly. She viewed herself from every angle in the tall glass and was satisfied she had never looked better in her life.

Fortunately, she was not in the habit of keeping her maid up to help her disrobe so there was no need to tell Jenny not to return that evening. Indeed, no one apart from herself was aware that her husband did not visit her nightly to perform his marital duties. Certainly, the nightgown she had been wearing was of the diaphanous variety, not plain cotton with a little lace at the collar and cuffs that she had been used to.

He was still in his own chamber. She could hear him moving about and the soft murmur as he discussed his apparel with his valet. The only jewellery she possessed was the emerald necklace and a long string of pearls. These would be perfect tonight and she waited for them to be threaded around her neck.

'Thank you, you may go now.' The girl was about to depart when Giselle decided to ask what had been making her normally sunny-tempered maid so quiet these past few days. 'Just a moment, Jenny, I wish to know what is bothering you. Are you unhappy being here with me?'

The girl burst into noisy tears. 'My lady, I am missing my Billy. We were walking out. He is an undergroom at Silchester Court.'

'Oh dear! I wish you had told me before this. I would never have asked you to come. I shall speak to Lord Rushton this evening and see if I can arrange for you to return so you can be with your young man.'

Instead of being happy at this, the girl cried even harder. 'I can't go back, I'd have no position. Billy doesn't earn enough for us to be wed. We are waiting for him to be promoted, then perhaps he can rent a tied cottage and get permission for us to marry.'

'I did not understand your predicament. I shall write at once to the duke and ask him to promote your young man so you can return to be married.'

Finally, the girl dried her eyes and sniffed loudly. 'Thank

you, my lady, I would be ever so grateful. Do you wish me to start training up a girl to take over from me when I do leave?'

'No, that won't be necessary.'

Giselle was about to go down when there was a soft knock on the communicating door. Her heart jumped. 'Please come in.'

The door opened and Rushton appeared. He looked magnificent in his evening clothes. He remained where he was until she beckoned him in.

'There is something I have been meaning to give you, my love, but until today I wasn't sure you would be happy to receive it.'

She was intrigued and waited expectantly to see what the gift might be. He held out his hand and she placed her left one in it. Slowly he unbuttoned her glove and peeled it off. Every brush of his fingers on her wrist gave her palpitations. Once this item was removed he slid a beautiful betrothal ring over her knuckle. The lustrous stone in the centre was an emerald that exactly matched the necklace she had already received from him.

'I shall remove my pearls at once and put on your necklace...'

'You shall do no such thing. The emerald in your ring matches your eyes and your necklace matches your gown. You look even more lovely than usual, my darling. I am so glad we decided to change tonight.'

She looked at her bare hand and then waved the gloved one at him. 'I can hardly go down as I am, my love, do you care to remove this for me as well?'

'It will be my absolute pleasure.' His voice was deep, sending flickers of excitement up and down her spine. Surely he didn't intend to... to... tumble her into bed this very moment?

By the time the second glove had gone every inch of her was sensitive to his touch and he had done nothing more than remove her gloves – he hadn't even kissed her.

'My God, don't look at me like that, darling, or we shall never get down to dinner and Cook and Frobisher will not forgive us.'

He pulled her hand through his arm and together they strolled through the house, through the drawing room and onto the terrace where the table had been laid with the best napery, crystalware and cutlery. The candles were lit and it looked like something from a fairy tale.

* * *

How he held back his passion he would never know. If he had his way this would be a very brief meal and there would be no dawdling in the drawing room for tea and polite conversation. He wasn't sure if what he felt was love or desire – but whatever it was – it was all-consuming.

There was no claret served with the meal tonight and they both drank lemonade. He scarcely noticed what he ate. He was sure it was all delicious, but his appetite had deserted him. When the final plate was removed, he threw down his napkin and stood up. It was her place to do this but he was tired of following the rules.

'I thought it might be pleasant to walk in the garden and watch the sunset over the water.'

'Forgive me, but I am feeling fatigued. Do I have your permission to retire?'

'You don't need my permission; you must do as you wish. I shall take a short stroll and then shall also retire.'

She nodded. Her hands were shaking. Was she regretting

her decision? He tried to smile but found it difficult to hide his disappointment.

'Good night, sweetheart, I shall see you at breakfast. Perhaps we could ride out together and I could show you more of the estate?'

Her muttered response was inaudible and he didn't like to detain her when she was obviously distressed. His instinct was to throw the nearest item as far as he could but he would not give in to his temper this time.

This was ridiculous – hadn't their problems been caused by not talking about their wishes? He strode after her and arrived at her side as she was about to enter her sitting room.

'Giselle, have you changed your mind? I will not come to you if you have. I shall wait until you are ready.'

She grabbed his arm making him jump. 'It is you who said you would not see me until tomorrow. I have not had a change of heart – it is you.'

His answer was to sweep her from her feet and shoulder his way into her apartment.

* * *

Giselle stretched luxuriously, loving the feel of her naked flesh against his. If she had known just how wonderful making love was she would not have hesitated for so long.

'So, darling, you are awake at last. Forgive me if I overstayed my welcome.'

She propped herself on one elbow so she was facing him. 'Are you not supposed to remain here? I did not know that was the custom.' His bare toes were showing at the end of the bed. 'Perhaps it would be best next time if you remained in your bed and I came to you. You are overlarge for this one.'

'I was about to suggest the same thing.' He threw back the covers revealing their nakedness. She should have been shocked, but she wasn't. How could she be after what they had shared last night?

He stood up, wrapped her in a sheet and strode across her bedchamber and into his own. She laughed when she saw his valet vanishing into the dressing room as if his tailcoat was on fire.

'I apologise, sweetheart, I didn't know the wretched fellow would be in here.'

'I am perfectly decent and I'm sure he has seen you as nature intended on many occasions.'

He leaned down so she could flick back the covers and then dropped her unceremoniously into the centre of the bed. His eyes were dark and his intent was obvious.

She should have stopped him – it was full light already – but when he looked at her like that she forgot everything but the joy of being his wife.

A considerable time later she was roused by the sound of water being tipped into the bath next door. There was no sign of her husband – he must have got up and left her to sleep. Tactfully, he had drawn the curtains around the tester bed. To her astonishment and delight he had also fetched her nightgown and bedrobe so she wouldn't be obliged to return to her own domain draped in a sheet like something out of Greek myth.

Once she was decent she pulled back the curtain and climbed out – it was a climb as the bed was considerably higher than her own. After checking she was unobserved she ran into her bedchamber and through to the bathing room.

Jenny greeted her with a smile. 'I didn't like to come and get you, my lady, not from next door. I hoped you would hear your bath being prepared.'

'Thank you, this is a treat indeed – to be able to bathe more than once a week.' She stepped into the lemon-scented water and relaxed. Jenny left her and went to set out her clothes for the morning. Then the door opened a second time. Had her maid forgotten something?

'I thought I would join you. It is high time that the master of this house enjoyed this newfangled room.'

She sat up so abruptly a cascade of water descended on the boards and he said something very rude when it covered his boots.

'Really, Rushton, that was quite unnecessary. If you had not come creeping in here and surprised me you would not have wet feet.'

'I don't think there is room for both of us, but I'm willing to try...'

He was now down to his shirt – she did not know a gentleman could remove his garments so speedily. 'You will do no such thing, sir; we have caused enough scandal amongst the staff for one morning. Kindly hand me that towel so that I may get dry.'

His smile was wicked and he held it tantalisingly out of reach. She stood up anyway, enjoying the way his eyes travelled from her toes to her crown in frank appreciation. She snatched the cloth from his unresisting fingers and, with a saucy smile, stepped around him and skipped into her bedchamber.

What Penrose and Jenny thought of him taking a bath at this time of the day she had no idea and cared less. She waited for him in her sitting room and her stomach was growling loudly by the time he came in.

'That was most enjoyable. I hear you are more than ready to break your fast, sweetheart.' His smile made her toes curl and she moved rapidly to the door before he could entice her back to bed.

'I am indeed sharp-set, my love, but it was ungallant of you to mention what you heard.'

'You have lost weight this past week and I intend to see you eat properly in future.'

He had his arm firmly around her waist and was hustling along the passageway at an undignified speed. 'Please, Rushton...'

'No, I refuse to have you use that name. In future I am Henry.'

'Is there anything else you wish to order me to do this morning, my lord?'

They were stopped at the head of the stairs and she was sorely tempted to give him a firm push in the small of his back but wisely thought better of it. He didn't deserve to break his neck for issuing orders.

'You are a baggage, my love, and I see I am going to be run ragged by you. I thought we had it perfectly clear between us – I am your lord and master and you are my obedient wife.'

'I don't remember that we had a great deal of conversation of any sort last night, my lord, and I would...'

'If you refer to me again as "my lord" I shall not be responsible for my actions.'

Her laughter echoed around the hall and he joined in. 'I'm afraid that I shall not be able to call you Henry, it does not suit you. However, I'm prepared to call you Harry instead if that would suit?'

Her comment was intended to be a jest but he smiled and nodded. 'Harry? Yes, that has a certain ring to it. I was never overfond of Henry. Today is the start of a new life for both of us, so I think that my having a different name is ideal in the circumstances.'

18

In perfect harmony, Rushton led her to the breakfast room where the sideboard was laden with chafing dishes containing an assortment of food ideal for breakfast time.

When he brought her a third plate she raised her hands. 'I could not eat another morsel. It was all quite delicious. I hope Cook has the good sense not to prepare a midday repast as I shall still be far too full.'

His snort of laughter made her pause. What had amused him at her expense this time? He nodded towards the tall clock that ticked contentedly in the corner.

'Good heavens! It is almost twelve o'clock already. Small wonder that you laughed at me, my love.'

He tossed his napkin aside, stood up and politely pulled her chair back for her. The fact that she was still sitting in it made her giggle. In fact, everything this morning seemed full of joy and humour. She was so happy she thought she might burst.

'Our daughters will expect to spend time with me this afternoon. I could not possibly play cricket today, not after eating so much. A gentle drive around the countryside would suit me perfectly. I shall ask for the chaise to be prepared.'

'No, I shall drive my family out today. We shall take the barouche; there is not enough space in your carriage for all of us.'

'That sounds delightful. Are we to dress for dinner again tonight?'

'I rather thought we could dine in our apartment in future. Do you have any objections to my suggestion?' She knew from the glint in his eye why he wished to do this and was tempted to refuse just to see his reaction.

'That will be quite acceptable. Are we to keep country hours in future?'

'If that is what you prefer, sweetheart, then I have no objection.' His smile was wicked. 'Are you to inform the kitchen of our plans? After all you have now assumed the responsibilities of the household.'

The thought of being obliged to give these particular instructions, knowing the reason behind them would be immediately obvious, filled her with dread. 'Maybe I could write a note instead? Which reminds me, I promised to write to my brother with regards to the young man my maid is walking out with. She wishes to return to Silchester but cannot do so unless he is promoted and can move into one of the tied cottages on the estate.'

His expression became serious. 'However much you wish to, my love, I don't think you should become involved in this matter. You're no longer residing there, and I doubt that the duke would take kindly to your interference. If you are dissatisfied with the performance of your girl, then by all means dismiss her and give her the money for her coach fare.'

She heartily wished she had not mentioned this to him as it

would now be a matter of contention between them. Whatever his thoughts, she had given her word and intended to write to Beau. Although she loved her husband to distraction, she was not blind to his faults. He was inclined to be dictatorial and over-punctilious about matters – in fact, he was almost a mirror image in personality of her oldest brother. Was that why she had been attracted to him in the first place?

'I must speak to Johnson. At what time shall we meet outside for our drive?'

'An hour from now. Good luck with your meeting.' His hateful chuckles followed her down the passageway as she walked briskly to the small drawing room that in future would be her study.

The consultation with the housekeeper went better than she had feared. When she informed Johnson of their future plans the woman merely nodded and jotted it down in her notebook.

'Would you require a simple meal, or several removes, my lady?'

'One savoury course and one dessert will suffice. That will be all this morning, thank you.'

There was ample time left for her to write her letter. She filled it with news of her happiness, extended an invitation for Beau to come and visit as soon as may be, and only mentioned Jenny in the last paragraph.

She sanded the paper, folded it neatly and sealed it with a blob of wax. Now all she had to do was work out how to get the letter in the post without her husband being aware of it. Then she decided to ask him to frank it. After all, he would expect her to write and tell her brother how things were progressing here.

Her fervent prayer was that he would just assume she had followed his instructions and had not mentioned the groom at all. If he asked her outright she would not be able to lie and would have to face the consequences.

The letter was handed to the butler and he said it would be taken to the posting inn later that morning with some other correspondence.

'Lord Rushton and I are taking our daughters for a drive shortly so it would not matter if this missive waited until tomorrow when he has time to deal with it.'

'His lordship has given me the responsibility of franking his mail, my lady, so I can assure you there will be no delay in sending this to his grace.'

'I have been wondering why we have received no morning callers – were my cards not sent out as requested?'

'His lordship wished them to wait until after the ball and the garden party, my lady.'

'In which case, delivering them will then be redundant. I will be able to talk to the people in person and can decide for myself whether I wish to further the acquaintance.'

* * *

Rushton walked from the house with a spring in his step. He was seeing everything with fresh eyes. After strolling to the stables to arrange for the carriage to be brought round he wandered into the woods to marshal his thoughts.

He came to the incredible conclusion that what he had felt for his beloved Charlotte bore no comparison to his feelings for Giselle. For the first time in his life he understood what romantic love truly meant. It changed everything. Even the sound of the birds was sweeter, the sky brighter and everywhere he looked he saw things he had never observed before.

Of course, he had loved his first wife, but it had been a

different kind of emotion. His heart had not soared when he caught sight of her, his every waking moment had not been filled with thoughts of her and their lovemaking had been enjoyable rather than spectacular.

How was it that he had been blind to his feelings for Giselle until now? Had he been waiting for her to grow up before he recognised that he had fallen in love with her? He flopped against the nearest tree trunk, his palms clammy, his heart thundering. If Silchester had ever suspected he had designs on his sister he would have broken his neck without hesitation.

He remained where he was for a while, breathing in the scents of the woodland until he had recovered his composure. He had not been mourning Charlotte for the past five years but using her death as an excuse to keep him safe from predatory matrons until Giselle was old enough for him to declare himself.

Would he have offered for her if her cousin had not created the situation? Allowing her to take charge of his daughters, when he was so protective of their well-being, had been so out of character he should have realised then. He pushed himself upright, ignoring the moss marks he had collected on his smart jacket he strode back to the house determined to show her in every possible way just how much he loved her.

Physical love was important, but there was so much more to it than that. He had deep pockets and intended to spend freely and indulge her every whim. Tonight, when they were alone, he would ask her when she had understood she was in love with him. He could never admit that he had lied to her, had married her under false pretences, as he doubted she would forgive him.

The carriage was waiting at the rear of the castle, the handsome team of matched bays tossing their heads, eager to be away.

'Papa, we have been waiting this age. Can we get in now that you are here?' Estelle said as soon as he was close enough to be spoken to without the child having to shout.

'You can, sweetheart. I apologise for keeping you waiting.'

Then his younger daughter grabbed his arm. 'Papa, you have green stuff across the back of your coat. Did you take a tumble in the woods?'

'No, I was leaning against a tree whilst I contemplated what a lucky gentleman I am to have two beautiful daughters and a beautiful wife.'

This statement pleased all three of them. Once the girls were settled on the squabs he lifted his wife onto the box and then jumped up beside her. He glanced over his shoulder at his daughters. 'You must promise me you will deport yourselves with decorum back there. Your mama and I are trusting you to be able to travel without supervision.'

They bounced up and down in excitement and gave their word they would be on their best behaviour. He flicked the whip over the heads of his team, released the brake and the carriage moved away smoothly.

'I thought I would take you to the village. We have a general store, a cobbler and blacksmith there as well as the posting inn. There is a weekly market in the square and it is held today, so there will be stalls of fresh produce, pins and ribbons and other knick-knacks for sale. I think the children will enjoy being able to purchase a few items for themselves.'

'I took the precaution of putting my purse in my reticule for just such an eventuality. By the by, do you like my new ensemble? It also has a parasol but I thought you might object to me using that in your carriage.'

He had not done more than think how lovely she looked, but now he gave her appearance further scrutiny. She was wearing a gown of striped material; her spencer was the exact shade of one of the stripes and her bonnet was lined to match. Even her reticule had been made to complement this outfit.

'A delightful confection, my love, and I am grateful that you refrained from bringing the parasol. I fear my team would have objected to such an object.'

'There are ominous black clouds on the horizon. I do hope we are not to get a drenching. The hood, when it is pulled up, will give the girls some protection but we are completely exposed sitting on the box as we are.'

'You are right, sweetheart. We shall curtail our drive. The village is only a couple of miles from Castlemere and we can spend an hour there before returning. I doubt the storm will roll in before then.'

* * *

They walked arm in arm around the square, nodding and smiling as his villagers touched their forelocks or dipped in a shallow curtsy. He allowed his daughters to wander freely amongst the stalls as he was able to see them over the heads of the crowd.

Giselle had gone to join the girls as they were disputing over some frippery or other when he saw one of his grooms dismount with the leather pouch in which his letters were conveyed back and forth from the inn.

The man bowed as he approached. 'Show me what is going today, Jenkins. I didn't see the pouch this morning.'

There were three business letters he had signed, but his secretary had written for him, two in the hand of his estate manager and one addressed to the duke. He frowned as he looked at it, but then dismissed his momentary worry and handed the letters back to the groom.

He forgot about what he had seen until they were home again and the girls had run off to show the governess their purchases.

'Giselle, I noticed you had written to your brother.' He paused, not sure if he should ask if she had followed his instructions as she would be offended by his lack of trust. Then he saw telltale spots of colour on her cheeks. 'Did you mention the matter of your maid?'

She straightened her shoulders, swallowed and looked at him directly. 'I did. I know you asked me not to, but a Sheldon never breaks their word.'

'You are a Rushton now, not a Sheldon, and as my wife I expect you to follow my instructions.'

'Are you suggesting that in future I must break my promises? That being your wife does not require me to be honourable?'

'Don't be ridiculous, you are twisting my words. Scarcely two weeks ago you promised to love, honour and obey and already you have broken that vow. Where does that fit into your peculiar view of morality?'

She curtsied in a parody of formality and his anger increased. It would not be sensible to continue this in so public a place. Before she could protest he gripped her elbow and marched her inside, not pausing until they were secure in his study with the door firmly shut behind them.

When he released his hold she rubbed her arm as if he had hurt her. That was ridiculous. Then he saw her eyes glittering and whatever he had been going to say was replaced by an overwhelming sense of shame that he had mistreated her.

'Show me. I should be horsewhipped for dragging you in here. I don't understand why I am constantly losing my temper at the moment. I can't recall having done so for years and yet I seem to be permanently veering from one extreme to the other.'

She held out the arm. 'There is nothing to see. I was exaggerating my discomfort. I shall not apologise for telling Beau and I do not wish you to apologise for mishandling me.'

'Remove your spencer so I can see for myself that I did not cause you harm.'

Once she had removed her gloves she began to undo the buttons that held the front together. He didn't offer to slip it from her shoulders. Her rigid stance warned him she was not ready to forgive him.

'Dammit to hell!' He couldn't keep back the expletive when he saw the clear imprint of his fingers on her arm. 'That was unforgivable. You have my permission to return to Silchester Court if that is what you wish to do after my behaviour.'

'I bruise easily. There is no need to look so stricken. Do you want me to go?' Her expression was watchful, giving nothing away.

'Of course I don't – I love you – but if you don't feel safe...'

Then she was in his arms where she belonged. 'I know you would never raise a hand to me, never hurt me deliberately. I love you too and my place is here beside you, being a mother to your girls.'

'I shall do better in future, my love. I give you my word as a gentleman I will never so mistreat you again.'

Her smile was radiant. 'I cannot promise that I will always be the obedient wife you appear to want. I have been brought up to think for myself and have no intention of becoming a milksop.' She stood on tiptoes and pressed her lips to his. It didn't matter what she said from that point on, he would have agreed to anything.

'However, I shall to be the best wife and mother I can. I promise to always love you and my dearest wish is to provide you with a son of your own – and possibly more daughters as well.'

He reached behind her and turned the key in the lock. 'Then we are in complete agreement, darling, and I suggest that we set about the task immediately.'

* * *

'Harry, we cannot make love in here in the middle of the day. What will your staff think?'

'They will think nothing at all as I do not intend for them to know.'

His breath was hot on her neck and his fingers busy undoing the buttons that held her gown together at the back. She had intended to refuse but her body was responding to his and she had no intention of stopping him.

* * *

A delightful time later she lay in his arms in her petticoats, and he in just his shirt, revelling in the pleasure they had been able to give each other.

'We must get dressed before someone comes to look for one of us.' She glanced at the overmantel clock and squealed in shock. 'Look at the time! They will be sending up our dinner in half an hour and we must be there then.'

She scrambled to her feet, ignoring his protest, and stepped into her discarded gown. He deftly refastened the buttons whilst she pulled on her stockings and tied the garters above her knees. 'I cannot put my hair up as it was. Half the pins have vanished on the floor somewhere – what shall I do?'

He ran his fingers through it gently pulling out the knots and tangles. 'I shall braid it for you, sweetheart, and then you can leave it like that. I don't give a damn what my servants think. They know better than to pass comment. I can assure you that they are loyal and anything they observe will never be discussed elsewhere.'

'In which case, from now on we can do as we please and not be bound by conventions. You may use immoderate language whenever you wish and I shall show my ankles to all and sundry.'

He chuckled and kissed the top of her head. 'You're right to reprimand me. I will endeavour to keep my bad language out of the house.'

As he pulled on his unmentionables and boots she found her half-boots and pushed her feet in. By the time she was more or less restored to her former appearance he had his waistcoat buttoned and his topcoat on. He held up his mangled neckcloth.

'This is beyond redemption. We shall return to our apartment as we are.' He grinned and her heart flipped. 'Let us hope we don't meet the girls, as they would be bound to comment on our extraordinary appearance and I doubt either of us could come up with an explanation that would suit.'

19

The day of the ball arrived and Giselle escaped to her sitting room in an effort to get away from the interminable bustle as the staff rushed about putting things in place for the big event. Rushton – no he must be Harry to her now – had done the sensible thing and taken himself out for the day. She would have gone with him but she knew she might be needed to answer queries from the housekeeper, so could not absent herself.

There had been no response from Beau to either her request for him to promote the undergroom or come for a visit. It was unlike him not to respond with alacrity and she hoped this did not indicate there was something untoward going on at Silchester Court.

She had just returned from inspecting the arrangement for tonight's supper when the door was flung open and her brother stepped in.

'Beau, I am so pleased to see you. That now explains why you didn't reply to my letter.' She rushed across and flung herself into his arms and he held her close.

'I thought I would come to the ball. I have brought Billy with me so he can spend time with your girl. She can travel on the box with him when we return if you so wish. Have you found a replacement yet?'

'I have not even thought about it. I believe there are one or two girls already employed here who might suit. I shall speak to the housekeeper when she next comes to see me.' She looked at him more closely and saw there was something worrying him. 'You did not come here just for the pleasure of attending our ball, did you?' She gestured towards the chair and he sat down with a sigh.

'You know me too well, sweetheart. I have had a letter from Perry's commanding officer. He is missing somewhere behind enemy lines and they fear for his safety.'

Her pleasure at his visit evaporated at his dreadful news. 'How long has he been gone? Does Aubrey know? He will be devastated if anything happens to his twin.'

'I've had no communication from Aubrey for several weeks. The last time I had a missive he and Mary were sailing towards Egypt.'

'What do Bennett and Madeline suggest?'

'They agree with me. I intend to go out to Spain and conduct a search myself. I'm hoping that a civilian might have better luck with the partisans than the soldiers that were sent to look for him.'

'Then you will be in danger also and I don't think Perry would wish you to put yourself in harm's way.'

'I have no choice, little sister. I would do the same for any of you. By the way, I heard from Lady Augusta, Lieutenant Sullivan's mama, asking me to give permission for Beth to become betrothed to her son.'

An Accommodating Husband

'And what did you reply?'

'I agreed. I know I said they must wait until next year, but I have no wish to stand in the way of her happiness. Word has been sent to his regiment and, if the colonel gives his permission, then I shall take Beth with me and deliver her before I begin my search.'

'She will be delighted to have you stand by her for the ceremony. Thank you for coming in person to tell me this bad news – I appreciate your doing so.'

'I can see from your demeanour that you are happy in your union. I would never have selected someone so much older than yourself, but I am happy that it is working for you both. Where is Rushton?'

'He is hiding from the chaos of the preparations. As the lady of the house I'm obliged to remain, otherwise I would have gone with him and not been here to receive you.'

She had been about to ring for refreshments when Frobisher appeared at the door. He bowed deeply – no doubt impressed by the presence of the Duke of Silchester at Castlemere – and ushered in two footmen carrying laden trays.

'I took the liberty, my lady, of bringing refreshments for his grace.'

'Thank you, I was about to ring.'

The trays were put on the table she used as a desk and then the servants retreated as quietly as they had come. There was enough to feed half a dozen let alone the two of them.

'Help yourself to food, Beau, and I will pour us both some coffee. I think Cook has sent us some of the things she has made for tonight. I can assure you a midday repast is not usually as varied or luxurious.'

They were happily devouring the delicious treats when

Harry strode in. As always, the sight of him made her pulse skip and she couldn't hide her joy at seeing him back so soon. He ignored her brother and came to her side. She tilted her face to receive his kiss. His lips were cold and hard and her bodice became unaccountably tight.

Beau cleared his throat noisily and her husband winked at her, making her giggle. He turned to face his brother-in-law. 'You are an unexpected but very welcome guest, Silchester. Forgive my poor manners, but I did not at first see you there.'

This was a blatant lie – they all knew it – but it served the purpose. Her brother was on his feet and the men shook hands. 'I cannot tell you how glad I am to see you both so settled in your marriage. I take it you are to join us for luncheon – there is certainly more than enough for three on these trays.'

Giselle excused herself when she had finished as she had seen Johnson hovering in the corridor not wishing to disturb someone so illustrious as a duke. She saw neither of them during the remainder of the afternoon as she was occupied with her daughters and other domestic details.

She tried to push the thought of her beloved oldest brother putting himself in danger on the Peninsula. He could have left the searching to those who were better equipped to do so. There was more behind his desire to do it himself than he was admitting. She was certain this plan to go abroad and look for Perry was because he found it lonely rattling around Silchester Court on his own now they all had left.

The journey would occupy him for a few months and with luck, and God's help, she prayed her missing brother would have returned safe and well long before Beau put himself in danger.

* * *

Rushton waited until his wife was safely away before turning to his friend. 'What has brought you here like this? It cannot just be a desire to see us.'

When he heard the story he understood at once that the duke had no option but to take on the responsibility for finding his missing brother himself. It was exactly what he would have done if he were in this position.

'When do you plan to leave?'

'Next month. This will give me months of decent weather to conduct my search. I'm sincerely hoping I shall find him long before winter sets in.' His expression changed. 'I did not tell Giselle the whole. The letter I received was penned as if Perry was already dead and buried. They are not looking for him as the information they have indicates he was shot when he came in contact with the French brigade.'

'That's grave news, I'm glad you didn't burden her with this. Do you have sufficient funds to cover your expenses and hire the local guides you will need for your endeavours?'

'I do, but I thank you for the offer. When Bennett married Grace her dowry replenished my coffers and since then I have had several business dealings bring in added revenue. I am well placed at the moment.' He paused and appeared to have difficulty continuing. 'If anything happens to me, the family will be thrown into disarray. Bennett has no wish to take on my responsibilities – as you know he was happier as a soldier than he has ever been living in my shadow. Could I ask you to step in and hold things together until the family have recovered from the loss of two of their members?'

'God's teeth! Do not talk of such a gloomy outcome. You must remain positive, my friend, and believe that your search will be successful and you will both return unscathed.'

'But do I have your word that if the worst happens I can count on your support?'

'You do – you know you do. But it will not come to that. You will return with young Perry at your side and all the family will gather and celebrate at Silchester Court when you do.'

He replenished their coffee cups and they sat in companionable silence for a while both lost in thought. There was something he needed to say and it was damned difficult to find the words.

'I want you to know, Silchester, that although when I married your sister I did not reciprocate her feelings, now I do. I believe I was always in love with her but it took me a while to wake up and grasp what was obvious.'

'Water under the bridge, old fellow, water under the bridge. All that matters is that you love her now. All my siblings have made love matches and I should have been sad to think that Giselle was the only one who hadn't.' He surged to his feet and headed for the door. 'Excuse me, I need to check my team has recovered from the journey and then rather thought I would thrash you at billiards if you are game for that?'

'An excellent notion. It will fill the space between now and dinner perfectly. Just a moment, Silchester, we are dining in our rooms tonight. The dining room has been changed to accommodate supper for the guests this evening.'

'What time do you expect the first arrivals?'

'Eight o'clock. A tray will arrive in your sitting room at six, which will give you ample time to change into your evening finery. I will accompany you to the stable yard. I'm sure you would like to see how the chestnuts you gave Giselle have settled in.'

* * *

Rushton returned to his shared apartment just as dinner was being placed on an impeccably laid table by the window in their sitting room. Giselle rushed in a few moments later.

'I am so sorry. I became involved in a riotous game of hide and go seek upstairs and could not possibly leave until it was over.'

She walked into his arms and he held her close. 'I have only just arrived myself, sweetheart, so we are both disgracefully tardy. I was going to suggest we sit down immediately but I think it might be advisable for you to remove the cobwebs and grime from your person before you do so.'

'If you insist, but as there are only ourselves to see my disarray I hardly think it matters.' She tipped her head to one side and put her hands on her hips like a fishwife.

'I will not allow your standards to slip so low, madam. You will get no food until you are respectable.'

'Pot, kettle, black.'

He scowled at her and she stuck her tongue out like a child and vanished into her bedchamber. She was right to point out that he was equally aromatic after his visit to the stables earlier.

Over the simple meal he began to explain what would be expected of her that evening, but she waved her fork at him.

'Harry, I have been attending balls all my life. I am well aware of the protocol involved. It is you who needs to be reminded how you must behave as this is the first ball held here for more than a decade, so Johnson tells me.'

He bit back his sharp rejoinder, not wishing to spoil the mood. He was not used to being spoken to so bluntly and eventually he would have to put her straight on this matter. But not tonight – this was to be a celebration of their love and their happiness and nothing was going to spoil it.

'That is quite correct; I hope you will forgive me for mentioning it, sweetheart, but I have been attending prestigious social occasions at the best houses in the country whilst you were still in the schoolroom.'

'Of course you have; I'm not a ninny. Also, there is no need to remind me of the age difference as I am well aware of that fact.'

His hands clenched. He had done the one thing he had hoped to avoid – upset her.

'One has only to look in the mirror to see that I am a beautiful young lady, a diamond of the first water, whereas you are a gentleman past your prime. Indeed, I expect you to demand the use of a bath chair at any moment.'

He leaned forward and tapped her on the knuckles with his own fork. 'Despite my imminent decrepitude, my dear, I guarantee that I can keep up with you.'

'I am sure of it, my love. I am wearing emerald green and I insist that you wear a waistcoat that complements my gown. I take it you have such a garment in your wardrobe?'

'Now you are being quite ridiculous. Why should a gentleman past his prime own anything but dull-coloured items?'

She put down her cutlery and rose gracefully to her feet. 'It will take me far longer than you to prepare so I must leave you now. I know it is customary for a couple to dance only twice together but I am sure the rules do not apply to those who are already married. I have arranged for there to be three waltzes as well as the other country dances. I wish to stand up with you for those.'

'I think I might manage to stagger about the dance floor three times without the need for resuscitation.'

Her delightful laughter filled the room and he wanted to go

after her and tumble her into bed regardless of the time. His valet was waiting for him in his bedchamber.

'Penrose, do I have anything of an emerald hue that I can wear tonight?'

'You have a fob, my lord, and a waistcoat with green and gold embroidery. They are set out for your inspection.'

'I will wear them, however disagreeable they might look. Do not wait up for me tonight. You may have the evening to yourself once I am dressed.'

The ball would not end until the small hours and even if he didn't intend to make love to his wife, it would be unfair to keep his man up so late.

* * *

Giselle had no need to examine her appearance in the glass; she knew she looked her best. Her husband was waiting impatiently in the sitting room to escort her downstairs. The first of their guests were already on the drive and heading for the castle.

His expression when he saw her made words unnecessary. She curtsied and he bowed. 'That is a handsome waistcoat, my love. I had no idea you had something so racy in your closet.'

He chuckled and touched her cheek with his ungloved hand. 'Penrose found this from somewhere. I didn't know I owned such a garment. You look enchanting. I cannot wait to introduce you to my neighbours.' His eyes twinkled and his smile was warm. 'I will be the envy of every man within twenty miles of here, for I guarantee you will be the most beautiful woman in the room.'

'And you will be the most attractive gentleman. I wish that my brother would make a push to find himself a bride. Beau will not be happy living alone in that vast house even with Bennett, Grace, Madeline and Grey so close. He is not enamoured of small children and my sister and sister-in-law are expecting a second happy event in the autumn.'

'Have you considered the possibility, sweetheart, that we might also be having an addition to the nursery next spring?'

'I should be delighted if we were. I'm hoping I can give you a son...'

'I don't give a damn if I never have a direct heir – I am perfectly content with daughters.'

There was no time to continue this interesting conversation as they were met at the bottom of the stairs by her brother looking, as always, magnificent in his black. All her brothers were tall, broad and handsome but Beau was undoubtedly the most splendid of the four.

She curtsied, smiled and nodded to so many strangers she had quite forgotten their names when the last couple drifted past.

'They are waiting for us to open the dancing, sweetheart. I sincerely hope you didn't decide it should be a waltz. That will scandalise the tabbies.'

'It is a country dance, which means we shall have to partner each other four times not three. I expect that will send the matrons searching for their smelling salts.'

'I care little for their opinion. You will no doubt have noticed that I do not wear those ridiculous white gloves. In fact, I insist that you remove yours before we go in. If we are to cause a scandal we might as well compound it by breaking convention and appearing with naked hands.'

His emphasis on the word *naked* made her catch her breath. Her hands were trembling too much for her to undo the pearl buttons. He dealt with the task as efficiently as he did everything else and then tossed the articles onto a side table.

She walked, leaning on his arm, head high, knowing that even if they were not the handsomest couple in the ballroom, they were certainly the happiest.

20

The remainder of the ball was a blur. Giselle chatted and laughed with any number of guests but could not recall what was said or to whom she spoke. She danced four times with her beloved and cared not for anyone else's opinion but his. Beau danced with her but then retreated to the card room. He was too wily to be caught by any mama hoping their daughter would catch the eye of the most eligible bachelor in the country this season. She forgot her anxiety about her missing brother and just enjoyed herself.

As the closing bars of the last waltz were played she looked at her husband. He looked as content as she was. When the final guest had departed the three of them retreated to her drawing room, which hadn't been used this evening. Here they were served coffee – which they all preferred – and a plate of dainty pastries. These hadn't appeared on the buffet so must have been made specially for such an eventuality.

She kicked off her slippers and tucked her feet under her bottom. The two gentlemen folded their long lengths onto adjacent chairs.

'I cannot remember enjoying myself so much as I did tonight. We must have been invited to more than a dozen supper parties, musicals and routs. I sincerely hope cards will be sent as I cannot remember anything about the dates or locations of these events.'

'You were the belle of the ball, my love. I think there will be many ladies wearing emerald green next time there is a ball in the neighbourhood.'

'I could not have worn it before I was married – it would have been too shocking. One of the many things I like about being your wife is that I can dress as brightly as a peacock if I so desire and no one will pass comment on it.'

He stretched out a slippered foot and gently nudged her ankle. 'I shall certainly pass comment if you appear in something any brighter than the gown you are wearing.'

She pursed her lips and put her finger to them as if considering his answer. 'I rather thought I should have my next ball gown made in poppy red. I shall also have the neckline much lower as I did not have nearly as much on display as most of the matrons present tonight.'

'Over my dead body.'

'And mine,' Beau chimed in.

She waved airily at her brother who, until a few weeks ago, had been her guardian. 'Fiddlesticks to you, Beau. I answer only to my husband and if he gives me permission to wear scandalous gowns then you shall have nothing to say on the matter.'

Both gentlemen laughed at her comment. She sipped her coffee and watched the two men she loved most in the world as they discussed the price of corn, the war against France and the recent enclosures of common land.

Their voices sounded far away and her eyelids drooped. She was comfortable where she was and there was no harm in sleeping for a while until they retired. How long she had been asleep she had no idea but hearing her name mentioned brought her back to consciousness.

'I must say, old fellow, I never thought to see you both as happy as you are now. I had grave reservations about your marriage. Although you assured me the fact that you didn't love my sister would be no barrier to her happiness, I thought she deserved better.'

It was an effort to remain still, for it to appear to both of them that she was still fast asleep when she had just had her heart broken. How could the man she loved have lied to her? If she hadn't just heard her brother say so she would never have doubted her husband's sincerity. Her marriage was a sham – she had believed every word he said because that was what she wanted to hear.

She sighed loudly, stretched out her legs and rolled upright. 'I apologise for having fallen asleep, gentlemen, but I shall leave you to your conversation and retire. No doubt I shall see you both at breakfast.'

The fact that she now slept in his bedchamber meant that when she closed the communicating door, and used her own bed, he would understand he was not welcome beside her tonight. He would never be welcome again. She could not ask her brother to take her back to Silchester Court as he was complicit in this deception.

There must be somewhere she could go where Rushton would not find her – he was no longer Harry to her – she would have to make her plans carefully and depart after the garden party. Leaving the girls would be the hardest part of her decision but they had Miss Gibbons to take care of them and the governess would never abandon them.

She was tempted to put the chair back under the door

handle but decided against it. If he did come in, which was unlikely, he would leave if she told him he was unwelcome. After carefully draping her beautiful gown over the rail put out to receive it, she dropped her soiled stockings, garters and petticoats into the laundry basket.

Her more utilitarian nightgowns were neatly folded at the back of her closet as she hadn't been wearing them recently. Safely garbed in voluminous cotton she climbed into bed. It would soon be dawn and the birds singing would wake her up. It hardly seemed worthwhile going to bed at all.

There were no tears; she was numb, hardly able to comprehend how her happiness had been taken away from her by her discovery of his perfidy. If only she had remained resolute and taken herself away to a little-known estate in Northumbria and not married him. She would have been sad for a few weeks but her heart would not have been in pieces as it was now. Neither would the girls be made so miserable by her departure.

With the curtains pulled tight around the bed she tossed and turned, trying to think of a way forward that wouldn't cause Estelle and Eloise so much pain. Children were resilient, more so than adults, and no doubt the two girls would soon forget about her and return to their usual happy selves.

Somehow, she had to get through tomorrow without revealing she had overheard Beau reveal that her husband was a liar and that he had married her under false pretences. But did it really matter that he had not loved her at the outset if he genuinely loved her now?

She pushed herself upright, knowing she was not going to sleep. She reviewed everything that had transpired between them and could detect no difference between his professions of love before they were married and those of the last few days.

She could not believe anything he said as he was a consummate liar, and so good an actor he could appear on the London stage.

When Jenny arrived with her morning chocolate and sweet rolls she was sitting at her desk in her sitting room.

'Good morning, my lady, and a lovely fine one it is going to be too. I did not expect to see you up so early as the ball didn't finish until two o'clock.'

'Put the tray down over there, if you please, I wish to finish writing my letter. When it is done, I wish you to walk down to the village and hand it in yourself. I shall give you the necessary coins to pay for the postage.'

If her maid thought this an unusual request, she kept her opinions to herself. Giselle sanded the paper, shook it clean, then folded it carefully and sealed it with a blob of wax. Then she wrote the address on the front.

It was fortunate that Rushton had so far shown no inclination to open her mail. She knew that some wives could not receive anything without their husbands having read it first. The missives that had come from Grace, Madeline, Beth and Bennett had all been handed to her by Frobisher unopened. Hopefully the same would happen when she got the reply from this note.

She now realised it would be impossible to leave tomorrow. She had to get her plans in place and this could well take a week or more. It would be impossible to keep him from her bed that long, but she thought she had come up with a solution. She would tell him her monthly flows had started and she preferred to remain in her own bedchamber alone until they were finished.

As they had not been intimate until a few days ago he would have no notion of her cycle and was too much of a gentleman not to take her word on the matter. Of course, if he asked, Jenny would know she was lying, but he would not do that. Now, all she had to do was get through today without revealing her intentions.

* * *

Rushton found his bed overlarge and empty without his beloved beside him. He understood her wish to get a few hours' unbroken sleep but hoped she would join him again tonight. Not just because of his desire to make love to her, but because when she was beside him he could listen to her breathing, know she was safe from harm.

Charlotte had never moved into his bedchamber; all the years they had been married he had visited her once or twice a week in her own room. It had never occurred to him to suggest otherwise.

He had slept surprisingly well and bounded out of bed eager to start the day by visiting his wife. He was about to walk through but paused and knocked politely on the communicating door. It opened and the maid curtsied.

'Her ladyship is in her sitting room, my lord, but she is not dressed.'

'I will go through. Put out her habit; we shall ride this morning before breaking our fast.' The girl curtsied and he stepped past her and walked into his wife's sitting room. He supposed it was really intended to be shared, but it had always been Charlotte's alone and he had no intention of changing that.

'Good morning, sweetheart, did you sleep well?'

She looked up and it was as if he was punched in the chest. There were black circles under her eyes, her cheeks were pale – in fact she looked as if she was sickening for something serious.

'As you can see, my dear, I am not myself today. There is no need for you to look so serious; it is no more than my usual monthly troubles. I intend to remain here until it is time for me to come down and greet the next lot of guests.'

The band around his chest slackened. 'Then you must rest. Forgive me for asking so personal a question, but do you always suffer in this way?'

She nodded and her cheeks coloured as if she found the subject embarrassing to discuss, even with him. 'I assume that you wish to remain in your own bedchamber for the next few days. Charlotte was incommunicado for the best part of the week. Will it be the same for you?' The thought of being alone for the next six or seven nights did not appeal.

'I am the same. I thank you for your consideration. I heard you telling Jenny to put out my habit. Forgive me, my dear, but I will not ride today.'

'Of course you won't. I shall find Silchester and go out with him. Is there anything you wish me to oversee this morning as you will be remaining upstairs?'

'Your staff are the most efficient I have ever had contact with and I am certain everything will be as it should without either of us having the need to interfere. I have sent word to the nursery that I am not available to see the girls this morning.' She smiled but for some reason her eyes were sad. Was she as disappointed as he was that she had not conceived this month?

'Then I shall leave you, darling, and occupy myself with your brother until you come down to join us.'

When he met the duke in the breakfast chamber his friend agreed a gallop across the countryside was exactly what they both needed to clear their heads.

'I'm surprised that my sister is not coming with us. She loves to ride, and the faster the better.'

'She is a trifle indisposed, but will be down in time for the garden party. I think she did not sleep well after so much excitement.'

Silchester looked at him askance and raised an aristocratic eyebrow. Devil take it! The man had misunderstood and thought the lack of sleep was for another reason entirely. Not something he wished to discuss with his brother-in-law.

* * *

As he was dismounting after an invigorating ride he saw his wife's maid hurry past. She had obviously been to the village on an errand for Giselle. He muttered something improper, which caused his friend to look round.

'I have not arranged for Giselle to have a monthly allowance. Did she bring any funds with her?'

'I've no idea, Rushton. I doubt that she spent all the pin money I allocated to her so I would expect she had several guineas in her escritoire. As you remained here until the day of your nuptials we have yet to sign the papers that will transfer her dowry to you. That's another reason I came in person. The necessary papers are in my luggage upstairs. We can deal with them tomorrow.'

'I don't want her inheritance, Silchester. Unless the documents leave the money with her, they must be redrawn. I have more than enough and would never wish her to think I had married her for monetary gain.'

He received a resounding slap on the back that almost floored him. 'Good God, man, you cannot do that. It would be unprecedented. My sister would not expect it. She is your wife, your responsibility – everything that was hers is now yours to take care of. Both my sisters are intelligent young ladies, but it is not for them to manage such matters – it is for a gentleman to take care of.'

Rushton shrugged. 'Then I shall take your advice and sign the papers before you leave.'

His grounds were filled with people busy setting up stalls and hanging bunting about the place. In the marquee that had been put up his staff were setting out the splendid buffet that was being provided for his guests, and there were a dozen or more barrels of ale already tapped and waiting to be drunk.

'I'm going to walk around and see what is being provided as entertainment for our guests. Giselle took me severely to task about my intention to provide only food and drink. I've no notion what has been organised.'

They parted company and made arrangements to meet up on the terrace at two o'clock when the event was planned to start. There would be no carriages arriving, or guests to be greeted in a line – his tenants and their families and the villagers would make their way, on foot mostly, although some might come in a pony cart, he supposed.

In fact, he had no intention of venturing onto the grass. They would do better without his supervision. The papers would have to be signed, but as soon as they were he would get his own lawyers to set up a trust fund so Giselle had control of it. She could then spend it on whatever she wanted and not feel beholden to him. He wanted her to be with him because she wished to be, not because she had no other option. In law she was his possession, had no legal rights, but he wanted to be an accommodating husband and do things differently.

21

The garden party was judged to be a resounding success by all who attended it. Giselle was relieved when Rushton said it would be better for them to depart and let his people enjoy themselves without constantly having to bow and scrape to them.

'Do the girls have to come inside as well?'

'No, Miss Gibbons is quite capable of overseeing their enjoyment.' He put his arm around her waist and it was all she could do not to flinch away. 'You do not look at all well, my love. Why don't you retire?'

'If you don't mind, then I should like to do so. I shall see you before you leave tomorrow, Beau, I hope?'

Her brother nodded. 'I'm going from here to London as I have documents to return to my lawyers, so there is no necessity for me to leave early.'

Giselle was pleased they had both accepted that she would not be joining them for dinner. There were things she needed to consider before she received a reply from her one-time governess, now Mrs Anderson, who resided in a village just outside Colchester called Great Bentley. This was ideal as it would be a simple matter to catch the stage as this village was also in Essex.

She and the erstwhile Miss Henshaw had remained friends and frequently corresponded even though they had not seen each other for more than four years. If she could not go there, then she would have to rethink her plans.

She entered the house through the terrace accompanied by her husband and brother. They had walked through the drawing room, and she was about to go upstairs, when a woman screamed. The sound came from the front of the house.

Rushton and Beau were out of the door, leaving her to run along behind. They could move far quicker with their long legs and lack of skirts to hold them back. This first heart-rending scream was joined by others and she realised at once what had happened.

A curious village urchin had been investigating the moat, which was weed-filled and several feet deep, and toppled in. By the time she arrived both her brother and husband had hooked off their boots, removed their topcoats and stocks were about to dive in to find the child.

There were now a dozen or more people gathered at the edge, attempting to offer comfort to the distraught mother. It would be better for her to remain on the bridge as her presence would not help the situation.

She watched both men vanish beneath the green surface in what she thought might well be a vain attempt to save the life of the little one who had fallen in. The child had vanished beneath the weeds and not come up again. This could not be good.

She inhaled and held her breath. They would all be safe as long as she could keep holding it. She prayed to the Almighty to intervene and bring a happy outcome. She wasn't sure how long a person could survive under the water before they drowned, but it couldn't be for much longer.

Her fingers gripped the stone. Her breath exhaled in a rush and still neither Rushton nor Beau returned to the surface. Then first her brother broke through the weeds and then her husband followed with the limp form of a little boy in his arms.

Willing hands took the child and then the men were heaved from the water. They didn't flop onto the ground grasping for breath but were both attending to the child in what she thought would be a wasted effort to revive him.

Rushton stood up holding the child by his ankles and he first shook him vigorously and then swung him back and forth. To her astonishment his extraordinary actions brought water gushing from the child's mouth and then his arms began to flail.

The boy was handed back to his parents amidst cheers and clapping from the assembled crowd. She had never seen anything like it. Her brother and her husband had risked their own lives to save that boy. They were heroes not only to her but to everyone else present.

Her feet moved of their own volition and she was running across the bridge and down the steps that led to the moat. Somehow, he sensed her coming and turned. He was plastered from head to toe in slimy green weed, his clothes were ruined but he had never looked better in her eyes.

He opened his arms and she flung herself into them. He held her close and in seconds she was as wet as he. 'I thought you all had drowned. I was never more scared in my life. Why were you all under the water for so long?'

He kissed the top of her head. 'The boy had become entangled in the reeds and it took both of us a while to get him free.'

They were now surrounded by his staff. A blanket was thrown about his shoulders, and no doubt the same was done for her brother, and in his stockinged feet, with his arm still around her shoulders, they returned to the house.

Frobisher glided up beside them, for once almost animated. 'My lord, I have arranged for the child to be freshly garbed and then he and his parents will be taken home. Hot water is being sent to your bathing room for yourself and a hip bath is being filled for his grace.'

'Thank you, I shall require brandy and coffee to be sent up to both of us in half an hour.'

She was surprised he hadn't released his grip of her shoulders but then she realised he was having difficulty remaining upright.

'Send for the physician, Frobisher. My husband is not well.'

If Rushton fell there was nothing she could do about it; she was not strong enough to hold him upright.

'Allow me, little one. I'll get him upstairs.' Her brother put his arm around Rushton's waist and together they got him safely to his bedchamber.

Penrose was waiting. 'If you would care to step aside, my lady, I will take his lordship's weight from you.'

She stepped aside and the two of them half dragged her husband into the bathing room. She retreated to her own chamber and Jenny fussed and tutted whilst removing the ruined gown.

'Will you put on a fresh ensemble, my lady?'

'I shall not go down again today so something simple will suffice.'

She didn't intrude whilst Rushton was being bathed by his manservant and, from the sound of it, at least two other footmen were assisting. Her brother would have gone to his own rooms to get clean and dry again.

After a while she was certain her husband was in his own

bed and she knocked on the door, intending to go in and find out why he had been so unsteady on his feet. There had been no sign of an injury so all she could think was that he had swallowed too much of the noxious water and somehow it had poisoned him. She dismissed this thought after a while because if the water was indeed poisonous then the child and her brother would be also afflicted. The door was opened by Penrose.

'Forgive me, my lady, but his lordship does not wish to see you at present. We are awaiting the doctor and you will be informed after he has visited.' The man bowed and closed the door in her face.

It would hardly be ladylike to remain with her ear pressed against the panelling in an effort to hear what was going on. Reluctantly she made her way to her sitting room where she paced the floor until Beau tapped on her door and looked around it. 'May I come in?'

'Are you well? Why won't Rushton allow me into his room? Do you know how he is? What did the doctor say?'

He took her arm and guided her firmly to the daybed. 'Sit down, Giselle, and I will tell you what I know.'

She did as he asked, her heart pounding at his grave expression. 'Is it very bad? Has he suffered from an apoplexy?'

'No, nothing like that. I knew he had been hurt but had no idea how serious the injury was. When he dived into the moat something caught him in the side.'

'But I don't understand – he was only in his shirt and breeches and there was no sign of an injury or blood anywhere on his person. How could he have been seriously injured when there was no blood?'

'It was the damnedest bad luck. There was a broken pitchfork sticking, prongs upwards, at the bottom of the moat and one of the spikes entered his body under his arm. Although he did not bleed from the wound the doctor fears it has done some serious damage to his internal organs. There is also a grave risk of it becoming putrid because of the dirty water.'

'I will not be kept from his side. I don't care what he wants, I am not a silly debutante who will have a fit of the vapours at the first sign of anything unpleasant.' She stood up and readied herself for an argument.

'Go to him, sweetheart. He will be the better with you at his side. I shall not depart as planned tomorrow; I shall wait until he is on the mend.'

He didn't need to say what they were both thinking. If her beloved husband died then she would need her brother to be at Castlemere. She didn't even know if the estate was entailed. If she was made a widow, would she and the girls be homeless?

She would not think such things. He would get better – he had to as she could not live without him. It didn't matter if he had lied to her, he had done it for the right reasons. She would remain at his side through sickness and health as she had promised in her marriage vows.

This time she didn't knock on the communicating door but walked straight in. She stopped so suddenly she trod on the hem of her gown and almost toppled on her face.

'I thought you were dying. And here you are sitting up in bed as if there is nothing wrong with you at all.'

'Come in, my love, why don't you? Who gave you that ridiculous information? If it was that fool of the doctor I will...'

'It was my brother. He is under the impression you are about to kick the bucket and has kindly offered to postpone his trip to Town so he can be here when the dreadful event occurs.'

He laughed and then winced. 'It hurts when I move, but

whatever you might have been told, darling, there is obviously no damage to anything important apart from my pride.'

He held out his hand but she refused to take it. Her terror at the thought that he was about to meet his Maker had turned to justifiable anger.

'If you had allowed me to come in none of this nonsense would have occurred.' She snapped her fingers and a shame-faced Penrose slunk in. 'You, go at once and speak to his grace and tell him Lord Rushton is perfectly well. He was misinformed about his condition.' The valet scuttled off. 'I take it your man was not lying when he told me you didn't want me to come in?'

'I thought you were unwell, sweetheart, and didn't want you to feel obliged to be at my beck and call when I had a perfectly good valet to take care of me.'

They were talking in circles and she was no nearer the reason why Beau had come to her believing his brother-in-law was on his deathbed.

'I don't understand how the physician who attended you could have got things so wrong. I thought that my brother had remained with you whilst you were being examined?'

'Of course he didn't; he had to go and bathe. If I had known what the wretched doctor was going to say I would have stopped him.'

'I was only given this news five minutes ago and came to your side immediately to find you in better case than I am.' It was as much his fault as the doctor's that he had caused both her and her brother a deal of unnecessary anxiety and pain.

'Giselle, please don't tap your foot at me. I might not be in danger of expiring but I cannot get out of bed or move without being in pain.' He paused to ensure he had her full attention. 'In case you have forgotten, when I emerged from the moat I could barely put one foot in front of the other. When you first came in looking so worried I made light of my injury.'

Her anger was now directed at herself. She was railing at him when he had done nothing but try and protect her from hurt. She ran to his side intending to embrace him but hesitated, not sure if he was well enough for her to do so.

* * *

Rushton braced himself for a shaft of pure agony as his darling girl came towards him. He was not being honest about his injury. He was painfully aware he would be incapacitated for several days, and possibly longer if anything untoward occurred.

'Sweetheart, there is nothing I would like better than to hold you in my arms but I fear that is not possible at the moment. I am not at death's door, far from it, but I did receive a serious injury.'

'Then I shall hold your hand but not sit on the bed. Did the doctor explain why your wound did not bleed when it is so deep?'

'He didn't, and I didn't enquire. The man is a fool and as soon as I am well again my first task will be to find someone else to attend the family. I hear that there is a young man who has set up a practice a few miles from here.'

'I don't think we should leave it until you are well; we must get him over here immediately. A second opinion could not go amiss, especially as the first one has been contradictory.'

He was about to protest that this would be better left to himself, but then reconsidered. Searching out this young physician would give her something to occupy her time until he was back on his feet.

'If Silchester is to remain with us for a while longer, get him to go with you. I don't like the idea of you gallivanting about the countryside in your chaise with only a groom in attendance.'

'I shall ask him when I see him later. I don't think the girls know about your accident – do you think I should go upstairs and speak to Miss Gibbons in case they hear gossip?'

'Do that, sweetheart. I need to rest for a while, but I should be delighted to see you again in a couple of hours.'

She raised his hand to her lips and kissed his knuckles in the same way he had done to her last night. 'I think your valet is hiding from me, and well he might. I believe he is jealous and resents the fact that you have married again so happily.'

'You could be right. I shall have words with him when you are gone.' She smiled and hurried out. The pain in his side was worse than it had been an hour ago and he was not sanguine about the outcome. He had denigrated his physician's prognosis but feared there might be more substance to this than he had at first thought.

Penrose hovered in the doorway. 'Fetch the duke.' Even saying so few words was difficult. Every breath he took was painful.

'There is no need, my friend. After speaking to your man I decided to come and see for myself how you were doing.' Silchester stood at the end of the bed looking down at him, his expression serious.

'There's another doctor in the next village. Will you fetch him to me?'

The duke snapped his fingers and Penrose moved into view. 'Stay with your master. Don't worry Lady Giselle. I shall be back as soon as may be.' Silchester stepped closer. 'Remain strong, Rushton. My sister and your daughters need you alive.'

He couldn't form the words to answer but blinked to show

he understood. The duke gently touched his shoulder and strode off.

When his valet offered him a large spoonful of laudanum he swallowed it gratefully. There was something very wrong with him and he feared he would not survive the night. As the opiate took hold he was able to drift off into a fitful doze. He wasn't given much to communicating with his Maker but he sent up a fervent prayer asking to be spared as he now had so much more to live for.

22

Giselle was on her way to the nursery when she heard heavy footsteps behind her. She glanced over her shoulder and saw it was her brother. 'What is it? Why do you look so solemn?'

'Rushton is far worse than we thought – in fact I think he is quite as bad as the doctor said earlier. I'm going to find another physician. I suggest that you don't speak to the girls on the subject, just send a message up to the governess asking her to keep them in the nursery so they don't hear about their father's injury.'

'I shall come with you. Rushton suggested we went tomorrow, but we can just as well go now. I will be but a minute or two to find a bonnet, gloves, cloak and put on my boots. I shall be down by the time the vehicle is ready to leave.'

In fact, she was down in advance of the arrival and was waiting under the portico when Beau drove through the arch to collect her. He had chosen the chaise as this was a carriage that could travel fast along narrow lanes.

Once she was settled beside him on the box he flicked the whip and sprung the team. He was an expert whipster and would not turn the carriage over. 'I take it you have the direction of the doctor we are seeking?'

'I do. Dr Gardner lives just outside Tunstead, which is three miles from here. I sincerely hope he is at home, not out on another call when we arrive. He can travel with us and can be returned home when he is done in one of Rushton's carriages.'

The chaise lurched as he turned the team sharply to the left as they exited from the drive. There was no danger of her flying from the box as she was holding on to the leather strap. She couldn't prevent the occasional sharp intake of breath as her brother negotiated several sharp bends with the team still cantering.

They thundered through the village, scattering a flock of indignant geese and causing several dogs to bark. The house they sought was on the outskirts, a substantial modern building in large grounds. Beau reined back so they could turn into the drive at a more sensible pace. Their approach must have been witnessed by a vigilant member of staff as there were two grooms waiting to hold the team, and the front door swung open.

A tall man in his thirties, with copper-coloured hair, dressed like any other gentleman of her acquaintance, emerged, a large black bag swinging from one hand. He took the steps in one leap and was at their side without pause. He vaulted over the door and the carriage rocked alarmingly.

'Why do you need me so urgently? Introductions can wait.'

'Good man. We are going to Castlemere. Lord Rushton needs your immediate attention.' Beau was unable to say more as he needed to concentrate on guiding the team safely through the gate and back onto the lane.

Giselle did not dare to turn around to give the young doctor any further information, and it would be pointless to shout as her words would be whipped away by the wind. They travelled back at the same reckless speed and were home in less time than it had taken to go there.

As soon as the vehicle lurched to a halt she scrambled down from the box, wishing to speak to the doctor and explain why he was needed. Beau had done what was required of him and the rest was up to her. Although she was at a loss to know why he had insisted she accompany him as he could have completed this task quite well without her. There was no time to ponder on this minor point.

She nodded to the doctor and together they hurried inside. 'I am Lady Giselle Rushton. The driver is the Duke of Silchester, my brother. My husband was impaled on the prong of an old pitchfork when he dived into the moat to save a village child.'

'I am Robert Gardner, at your service. Did the wound bleed?'

'No, hardly at all. He seemed quite well initially but has taken a turn for the worse.'

'You are fortunate, madam, that I am recently returned from six months on the Peninsula. I am a surgeon as well as a physician. I am certain I know what is causing your husband to deteriorate so alarmingly.'

They had reached the bedchamber and she opened the door and gestured him through. She was about to follow but he closed the door firmly in her face – this was the second time she had been excluded in this way. However much she might wish to be of assistance, if Rushton was to undergo surgery then she would be of no use to him as she became queasy at the sight of blood.

'I'll stay with him. I have a stronger stomach than yourself and Rushton would not wish you to see him suffer,' her brother said softly.

She turned to go into the sitting room but he called her

back. 'Wait downstairs. I will come and find you when there is any news.'

He was right to send her away, out of earshot, and let Dr Gardner take care of matters. She knew little about surgery but was fairly sure anything of that sort was dangerous to the patient. Remaining inside was not an option, but neither was walking around the grounds as they were still heaving with people enjoying the free food, drink and entertainment.

She was certain reports of their mad ride would be circulating already and she had no wish to be questioned on the subject. If their guests were aware how grave the situation was, their pleasure in the day would be ruined and they would go home dispirited. She was sure Rushton would not wish this to happen and neither did she.

It was getting dark but the jollity outside continued unabated. The trestles and benches would have been cleared from the marquee and now there would be dancing. The event would be brought to a close at midnight, but until then she must endure the sound of people laughing and clapping whilst she waited in terror of what might be happening upstairs.

* * *

From a distance, Rushton could hear two voices, one he recognised and one he didn't. Then a face swam into his vision and he did his best to focus and understand what was being said to him.

'My lord, you have the end of the prong lodged inside of you and that is what is making you so ill. It is why the wound didn't bleed. I'm going to remove it.'

Remove what? Who was this man? He was past caring and must leave whoever was speaking to him to do whatever he wanted. Despite the pain and difficulty in breathing he was still alive and intended to remain so.

'Do it,' was all he could manage and then busy hands removed his pillows, his nightshirt and the cover over his legs. He was then lifted and something dragged beneath his body. There was a clatter of metal and then a glass was pushed against his lips.

'Drink this, Rushton, you will need it. Better you pass out from alcohol than pain.'

Obediently he swallowed but he could take no more than three mouthfuls as the pain was too intense. His head was gently placed flat on the mattress. What felt like a piece of leather was pushed between his teeth. He knew what this meant – he was expected to bite down and not scream out during the procedure.

Something cold touched his side. A shaft of agony ripped through his body and then everything mercifully went black.

He came to as the doctor finished bandaging his chest. He was in pain, was weak and dizzy, but could swallow and breathe normally. He forced his eyes to open.

'Thank you. You found it.'

'I did, sir, and just in time. If it had been left inside your body much longer it might well have migrated to your heart. You have lost a deal of blood during the operation, but I've stitched you up and I'm hopeful of a happy outcome.'

'Not as hopeful as I am.' Penrose held a silver goblet, of what smelt like wine and water, to his mouth and he drank it greedily. When he was offered a second this too followed the path of the first.

'Excellent, my lord, the more you drink the quicker you will replace the blood you have lost. I shall remain here overnight in case you have need of me but now I shall leave you to sleep.'

The pillows were now back behind his head and Rushton relaxed into them. Time enough to speak to his friend and his wife when he was feeling more the thing.

He drifted in and out of consciousness all night but Penrose remained at his side throughout. His valet helped him onto the commode when necessary and then restored him to the comfort of his bed. At some point he was sure Giselle came in to see him and also at least twice the doctor was there checking his pulse and his bandages. Every time he woke he drank more watered wine and by the morning he was in his cups and incapable of coherent conversation or thought.

He was roused from his alcohol-induced slumber by his wife. 'Rushton, Dr Gardner has pronounced you out of danger and he has been returned to his home. He intends to visit you this evening.'

Blearily he opened one eye to see her smiling down at him, looking even more delectable than usual. He attempted to take her hand but for some reason his limbs refused to obey his instructions. 'Dammit, worse than I thought. Had a gallon of wine and am decidedly bosky.' There appeared to be two of her and she, for some benighted reason, was jigging from side to side in a most upsetting way.

'I shall leave you to recover, my dear, but wished you to know that your daughters send their love. I shall not allow them to come and see you until you are more yourself. I told Beau there was no need for him to stay an extra night, so he is now on his way to London.'

He closed his eyes and the next time he awoke his head was clearer. The pain in his side was no more than a dull ache and he thought he could get out of bed to relieve himself without ringing for Penrose.

An Accommodating Husband

'Just a moment, my love, please do not try to get out of bed on your own.' His wife emerged from the shadows.

'I can manage perfectly well, Giselle. Kindly remove yourself.'

Instead of going, she laughed. 'If you swing your legs to the floor, I shall pass you the necessary receptacle. Then I shall "remove myself", as you so politely put it, until you are done.'

He accepted the chamber pot with bad grace but his need was urgent and there was no time for argument. He was damned if he was going to hand his wife a brimming pot to empty. When he was done, he would push it under the bed and leave it for the chambermaid to deal with in the morning.

This task was accomplished but it was with some difficulty he heaved himself from his knees and back into bed.

'Let me help you. Why is it that gentlemen are so reluctant to accept that they need assistance? You make the very worst of patients.' She lifted his legs from the floor and put them under the cover and then plumped up his pillows. 'Do you need any laudanum? Anything to drink or eat?'

'No, no and no. What I do need is for you to return to your chamber immediately. If you wish me to sleep I shall only be able to do so when I know you are where you should be – in your own bed.'

'Your valet will be back at dawn so I think it's safe to leave you now. Sleep well, my dear. We shall talk in the morning. Our daughters are desperate to see their papa and I have told them they may come in after lessons.'

'I do not wish to see you here before midday, sweetheart. You must remain in bed and get a good night's sleep.'

'I'll endeavour to do so. Goodnight, my love, sleep well.'

* * *

Giselle fell into bed exhausted by her long vigil at her husband's bedside. She was satisfied he was going to make a full recovery and for that she was profoundly grateful. All thoughts of leaving him had been forgotten and, as she fell asleep, she recalled that she must write to her erstwhile governess first thing and cancel the request to move in with her.

The rattle of her curtains being drawn back and the shutters being opened eventually roused her the next day. She sat up, blinking in the bright light, realising at once she had slept in as her husband had demanded.

'Jenny, what is the news from next door?'

The girl turned a beaming face to her. 'The master is well. That young doctor has visited and said he's going to make a complete recovery.'

'That's excellent news.' She did not query how her maid knew such details; it was a sad fact of life that one's servants knew as much about one's business as oneself.

'After my ablutions, I would like to put on something I've not worn before. It is possible I will receive half a dozen morning callers as I doubt that our neighbours will be aware Lord Rushton was seriously injured yesterday.'

The tray was placed across her lap and she tucked in with relish. There were coddled eggs, coffee, buttered toast and a selection of freshly baked pastries. Exactly what she needed as she had not eaten since she broke her fast yesterday.

'I wish you to make sure that Johnson is aware there might be visitors. If they arrive before I am ready they must not be turned away but sent to the drawing room and served with tea and almond biscuits.'

'I'll go down straightaway, my lady, and be back to help you dress when you have finished your breakfast.'

Once she had eaten Giselle jumped out of bed eager to

begin the day – far too much of it had been wasted by sleeping already. There was hot water in the dressing room and she was quite capable of washing herself without the assistance of her maid.

The gown she selected was pale green muslin with dark green flowers embroidered on it. The sash under her bosom was the same shade of green as the flowers. It was a simple but elegant creation. Jenny arranged her hair to her satisfaction and she was ready to go next door and see her husband.

The communicating door was ajar and she walked in without knocking. Her brother was lounging on an armchair nursing a delicate porcelain cup in his hand. Her husband was propped up in bed and greeted her with a smile that curled her toes.

'At last, we began to fear you were going to sleep all day. That is a delightful confection you have on, my love, but it is wasted on us. Are you expecting a plethora of visitors?'

'I've no idea, but there could be several of the ladies I was introduced to at the ball arriving imminently so I cannot dally here. I just came to see for myself that you are well.' She smiled at Beau. 'I thought you had left for London and yet here you are.'

'I have postponed my journey until tomorrow morning.' He jerked his head towards the window. 'If I'm not mistaken, I can hear the sound of a carriage arriving. You had better hurry downstairs so you can greet the first of your morning callers.'

'Have the girls been in to see you yet?'

'I have had word from the nursery that they will be coming shortly. I am assured it will be a brief visit, for which I'm grateful. I might look more robust but I'm still as weak as a kitten.'

She could hardly dash across and kiss him when her brother

was in the room so she contented herself with another smile and left them to their masculine conversation.

Her assumption that she might be inundated with callers was correct as a constant stream of visitors drifted in and out of the drawing room. By the time the last one left at three o'clock she was heartily relieved. Everyone had been shocked to hear how poorly Rushton had been and praised him for his bravery.

The fact that her husband was confined to his bedchamber allowed her the freedom to excuse herself from returning calls for at least another week. Apart from discussing the near drowning and heroism of her brother and husband, all her visitors had been interested in was hearing about her brother. It had not gone unnoticed that the Duke of Silchester as yet remained unmarried. Beau had very wisely remained invisible all afternoon.

Unfortunately, there had not been a single person who had come to call that she wished to further her acquaintance with. She had hoped there might be other young ladies like herself, recently married, and who might be interested in things apart from the latest gossip, the latest fashion and the next social event they were going to attend.

She ran up the stairs and tapped on Rushton's door. Penrose opened it and put his finger to his lips. 'His lordship is asleep, my lady. Are you going to come in and sit with him until he wakes or do you wish me to fetch you then?'

'I shall be downstairs in my sitting room for the remainder of the afternoon. Send word to me there when he wakes.'

She had yet to write the letter to Mrs Anderson and that could not be put off any longer.

23

Giselle went in search of her errant brother and found him lurking in the billiard room. This was not a place ladies frequented as a rule, but at Silchester Court the family had not followed such rules.

'You were wise to remain in here, Beau. There are at least half a dozen hopeful young ladies came visiting this afternoon.'

'From your demeanour, little sister, I gather Rushton is doing well.'

'He is asleep, but vastly improved. Thank you for remaining an extra night; it is much appreciated by both of us. Shall we dine on the terrace this evening as the weather is so clement?'

'I thought you would wish to eat with your husband but I should much prefer to have company. Don't rush off, stay and play a few frames with me.'

She could hardly refuse as he had been kind enough to stay until matters were improved. 'Your height gives you an unfair advantage, brother, so I shall need to be given a three-frame lead to make this match more balanced.'

He wasn't taken in for a minute and laughed. 'You do not

gull me so easily. Last time I agreed to such a thing you beat me by seven frames. You play as well as any gentleman of my acquaintance – in fact better than most. Have you challenged Rushton yet?'

'I haven't, but as soon as he is well I will do so.'

They spent the remainder of the afternoon in the billiard room and she lost by a narrow margin. They agreed they would not change for dinner so had played until a footman was sent to announce the meal was served.

After eating they both joined Rushton in his bedchamber and remained there until he became fatigued. Her brother bade them both goodnight and departed for his rooms.

'Is there anything I can fetch for you, my love, before I retire?'

'Nothing, thank you, sweetheart. The doctor is visiting tomorrow and I shall ask him if I'm allowed to get up. I find I am capable of walking without dizziness now and have scarcely any pain.'

'In which case I don't think you need his permission. You could put on your bedrobe and spend the day in our sitting room. Then the girls and I can visit you more easily.'

He agreed this was a sensible solution. He held out his hand and she went willingly into his arms. Considering he had been at death's door so recently his arms were strong and his kiss as passionate as ever.

A pleasurable time later she pushed against his chest and he immediately released her. 'You must not tire yourself, my dear. I shall see you in the morning – sleep well.'

* * *

She was up early and decided to go for a ride. Beau was ready to leave when she returned. They embraced fondly and he promised he would return immediately if anything untoward should occur and then he departed for Town.

To her delight her husband was dressed and waiting for her in their sitting room. 'Good morning, darling girl, I have ordered breakfast to be served in here for both of us.'

She stepped around him, not wishing to be kissed when she reeked of the stable. 'I shall be but a minute. I must wash and change before I join you.' She paused at the door. 'I believe we agreed that you would not get dressed but remain in your night garments.'

'You suggested it, sweetheart, but I don't remember that I actually agreed. I have never sat about in my nightshirt and have no intention of doing so today. However, until Dr Gardner tells me that I may, I shall remain in our apartment not venture anywhere else.'

It was highly unlikely he would do whatever the physician said unless he agreed with it. With Jenny's able assistance she was back in the sitting room in a simple dimity morning gown in less than a quarter of an hour.

Their repast had been laid out on the sideboard in silver chafing dishes as if a dozen or more were expected to eat. The coffee jug was already on the table along with the necessary crockery. Rushton was seated at the table looking expectantly at her.

'I suppose in the circumstances I am prepared to serve you – do not become accustomed to it, sir. What would you like me to bring you?'

'Until I know what the kitchen has sent up, my love, I cannot possibly say what I want.' He smiled sweetly and she scowled at him.

'You are getting a little of everything and will eat what you are given. I've no intention of peering into each container more than once.'

He raised his hands and shrugged. 'Let us compromise, I shall have whatever you are having.'

She was tempted to give him toasted bread without either butter or conserve but thought that would hardly be fair. Everything looked and smelled delicious so she piled his plate with a miscellany of eggs, ham, mushrooms and, for good measure, a large dollop of kedgeree. She then served herself a similar plateful and carried them to the table.

Neither of them had eaten yesterday and both ate heartily. They drained the first coffee jug and were halfway through the second before they declared themselves replete.

'I shall ring for someone to clear this away. I thought perhaps we could play a game of Piquet or Whist – or do you wish me to fetch you something to read from your library?'

'I've no wish to play cards with you, sweetheart; I would much prefer to talk. It is true that we have known each other for years, but our relationship was quite different then. I wish to know what interests you and how I can make you happy.'

* * *

The doctor pronounced him well enough to remain upstairs but not to venture any further until the stitches were out and there was no danger of a putrid infection. Rushton had no wish to keep his wife at his side when the weather was so fine.

He could hear her playing on the grass outside with their daughters and went to watch through the window, wishing he could be out there with them. Giselle was leaping about with as much enthusiasm as the girls; even the governess was joining in.

Miss Gibbons must have volunteered as she was normally given the afternoon free from responsibilities.

The window seat was a tad short but he settled onto it as best he could, so he could continue to observe his family. He mulled over the past few days and something odd occurred to him. His wife had told him she was indisposed this week and yet here she was dashing about the place obviously in the best of health.

His lips curved ruefully. It was best if she didn't come back into his bedchamber at the moment as making love was something the doctor had told him must be postponed until he was fully fit. It would be impossible to lie next to her and refrain from such activities.

They finished their game and headed in the direction of the maze. He heaved himself from his prone position and rang the bell.

'See if there's been any correspondence delivered today. Also there should be yesterday's *Times*. Fetch them for me.'

His valet bowed. 'Shall I bring you some coffee and pastries, my lord?'

'I have barely recovered from my breakfast. The post and the paper will suffice.'

There were half a dozen letters. He smiled when he saw that only two were addressed to him and the others were for Giselle. He had no intention of opening them. He respected her privacy, but he was curious to see from whom they'd come.

There was one from her sister, one from her sister-in-law – he recognised the impression on the seals. He had seen her cousin Beth's appalling handwriting before and recognised it – but this left the other one. Who else would be writing to his wife?

He held this letter up to the light in the vain hope he might be able to decipher some of the contents and inadvertently touched the blob of wax, which broke off leaving the letter unsealed. It went against everything he believed to open it but boredom and curiosity made him carefully unfold the paper.

My dear Lady Giselle,

I was delighted to hear from you but deeply saddened and shocked by the contents of your letter. You give no details; these can be told when you arrive. Your husband must indeed be a reprehensible gentleman for you to wish to leave him so soon after your nuptials.

Come to me as soon as you wish – there is always a home here for my favourite pupil.

My very best wishes,

Emily Anderson

He stared with incomprehension at these words. They made no sense to him. He collapsed onto the nearest seat to gather his thoughts. She must have written this several days ago for there to have been a reply today. He remembered seeing her maid returning from the village on the day of the garden party.

What had he done to make her wish to run away? He should be angry – send for her and rage at her disloyalty, at her betrayal – but instead he was devastated. Now he understood why she had given the excuse to remain from his side. She would hardly wish to be intimate with him when she was about to... about to... he couldn't bring himself to even think the unthinkable.

He had believed her love to be genuine and yet this must show the opposite. He was unmanned by the knowledge that the woman he loved above anything else in his world did not return his feelings and intended to abandon him and his girls.

He closed his eyes and went through everything that had

happened that day. Then he understood. She had overheard Silchester when they were discussing the reasons for the marriage. She knew he had lied about loving her, that she had been deceived by both of them.

His cheeks were wet. At that moment he wished he had died from his injury, as to live without her was too awful to contemplate. Not for one minute did he consider trying to persuade her to stay. His actions had destroyed their marriage and he must live with the consequences. He had told Silchester that if ever Giselle discovered his perfidy she'd not be able to forgive him.

She must never know he had read her letter. Like an old man, he pushed himself from the chair and went across to her escritoire to find a wax stick so he could reseal the message. A candle was always left burning for such an eventuality and it was a matter of moments to replace the broken wax with a fresh blob. He waved the letter back and forth until the seal hardened and then placed it between the other letters she had received.

He was too dispirited to open his own correspondence and left that on the silver salver with the others. He made his way back to his bedchamber and called his valet. 'I am feeling unwell and wish to return to bed. I do not wish to be disturbed by anyone apart from Dr Gardner.'

Penrose had more sense than to comment and helped him disrobe in silence. When he was safely under the covers he asked for the curtains to be drawn around the bed. If Giselle came in she would know at once he didn't wish to be disturbed.

* * *

Giselle saw the young physician waiting on the doorstep; presumably he wished to speak to her. 'Forgive me, my loves, I must go inside. I shall come to the nursery before you retire.'

They were intelligent girls and had seen the reason for themselves why she was leaving them. She smiled at the governess and hurried across the vast expanse of grass to the doctor.

'I'm sorry to drag you away from your children, my lady, but I need to speak to you about Lord Rushton. I am most concerned about his health – he has retired to bed, his cheeks are pale and his pulse erratic. I fear he is sickening for something.'

'He was perfectly well this morning. He was dressed and ate a substantial breakfast with me. How can he have deteriorated so suddenly?'

'It's a mystery to me. I've treated many similar injuries and once the first twenty-four hours have been survived the patients continue to make a good recovery. I've never seen a situation like this. Could I prevail upon you to go in and speak to him as he remained silent throughout my examination?'

'I shall do so at once. I'm at a loss to understand why he should be so taciturn. Do you think I should send for the duke?'

'It has not come to that, my lady, but I shall return this evening and see how he is. If he continues to sink in this way then I shall have to reconsider that decision.'

When she attempted to get into Rushton's bedchamber she was refused entry by his officious valet. 'Forgive me, my lady, but Lord Rushton was most specific that he did not wish to see anyone apart from the doctor today.'

She could hardly push the man out of the way but was tempted to do so. 'Then I shall respect his wishes. Dr Gardner is returning later today but you must inform me if there is any change in his condition before then.'

The man nodded but said nothing and closed the door. She wandered disconsolately around the sitting room picking things up and putting them down without being aware of what she was doing. Then the second time she picked up the silver tray she realised there were half a dozen unopened letters waiting to be read.

She put aside the two addressed to her husband and then eagerly read the news from Madeline and Grace. Beth had found another young lady who was going out to join her future husband and intended to travel with this person and her chaperone. Beau was going to London to set his affairs in order before he departed for the Peninsula to look for Perry. He would obviously now be escorting two young ladies instead of one and she hoped he would not object to this cavalier arrangement made by her cousin.

She came to the fourth letter and opened it without looking at the handwriting on the front. When she read the contents, her heart flipped – she should have written to Mrs Anderson but she had quite forgotten.

She would write her reply immediately and apologise for not having communicated her change of heart before this. Perhaps if she invited the older governess for a visit later in the year this would make up for her rudeness.

When she had finished writing she picked up what should have been a pristine stick of wax and saw it had been used. Puzzled by this she examined it more closely. Then she saw two small pieces of dried wax amongst the detritus on her escritoire.

She turned the letter from Mrs Anderson over and saw at once that the seal she had just broken had come from the wax stick in her hand. She dropped both items and raced to the communicating door. She didn't knock but burst in and ran to the bed.

She threw back the curtains. 'Harry, I am not leaving you. I love you and don't care that you married me under false pretences.'

He opened his eyes and she saw a spark of hope in them. 'You forgive me for lying to you?'

'I did so two days ago. It serves you right for reading my correspondence.' She had intended to say something loving, reassuring, but these words had popped out of her mouth of their own volition.

Before she could react, his arms shot out and she was tumbled head first into the bed.

'I could not live without you, my darling, but I would not have prevented you from leaving if that's what you'd wished to do...'

She wrenched herself from his grasp. 'I can't believe what I'm hearing. You would have let me go even though you say you cannot live without me? You would have made no push to persuade me to change my mind?' She scrambled from the bed and stood glaring down at him. 'I thought I had married a gentleman similar to my brothers, but it seems that I'm sadly mistaken.' She was warming to her theme and did not see the warning signs. 'Perhaps I will leave after all, for I do not wish to remain with someone who is so weak...'

The gentleman she was berating for being a milksop transformed into a formidable and dangerous opponent.

'You will be silent, madam. I will not be spoken to like that by anyone, and especially by my wife.' From being prostrate with grief on his bed he was out of it and standing far too close. Then an insane desire to giggle overwhelmed her. She put her hands across her mouth to hold it in but she could not.

His eyebrows rose so high they vanished beneath his hair and his eyes widened. 'I beg your pardon, my lord, but it is hard to take you seriously when you are standing there in your nightshirt with your hair in disarray.'

The matter hung in the balance for a second and then his mouth curved reluctantly. 'So, my love, not only am I a weak man, I am also a figure of fun?' His tone was bland; she was not fooled for a moment. She was due to receive her comeuppance if she did not remove herself smartly from his reach.

Her rapid move backwards was not prevented, which surprised her. Then he swayed and put his hand to his injury. He was unwell. She didn't hesitate but rushed to his side.

'You should not be out of bed. Let me help you return – or shall I call for your valet?'

His arm went around her shoulders and his knees almost buckled. Then, miraculously it appeared, he recovered his strength and tossed her onto the sheets. She was pinned down beneath his considerable weight.

'I can see that you are under a misapprehension, my darling, and I intend to rectify that immediately.' These words were more growled than spoken and she understood his intent immediately.

'You cannot – you must not – Penrose could come in at any moment.'

He rolled away but kept her in place with one arm across her chest whilst he flicked the open curtains back so they were cocooned in the gloomy interior of the bed.

This was a game they were playing and she could stop it any time she wished. It was up to her if this continued to its inevitable conclusion. Her skirts were rucked up exposing her bare legs and there was far more of him on show than was seemly.

'Do you recant your words? I demand an immediate apology.' He was lying beside her, his head supported on his hand. His words sounded fierce but his eyes said differently.

'I shall apologise for laughing at you but not for being angry that you would have let me go so easily.'

His expression became serious. 'I should not have lied to you, but I did it for the right reasons. I could not allow you to ruin your reputation. I believed that there being love on one side would be sufficient to make this a happy union.'

'And now?' She held her breath knowing that whatever he said would be the truth this time and she couldn't bear to think that he had been deceiving her this past week.

'I love you in a way that I never thought possible. I understand now that my feelings for Charlotte were more affection, and not true romantic love. What I feel for you is all-consuming, overwhelming, which is why when I thought I had lost you I could not think coherently.'

'But you would have hidden in here in your misery and allowed me to go?'

'I would not have let you leave. I was temporarily incapacitated, that is all. I blame the opiates I have been consuming for my uncharacteristic behaviour.'

'Then I shall apologise for calling you weak, for causing you a moment of unnecessary distress. But I will not do so for laughing at you.' She sat up and then turned so she was kneeling beside him. 'I do not like this garment you have on. I much prefer to see you as nature intended.'

His eyes blazed then he too was on his knees, there was a flash of white cotton and he was naked. She was about to begin the laborious process of undoing the buttons at the front of her gown when he took matters into his own hands.

'Too slow. Allow me to remove this.' He gripped the front of the bodice and ripped it apart, leaving her in her petticoats. There was little point in protesting as she was as eager as him to be unclothed. Her petticoats went the same way.

Then she froze and jerked away from him. 'Your wound is bleeding. I think you have torn a suture free.'

He glanced down at the trickle of blood. 'I shall recall the doctor – but it can wait until afterwards.'

'You shall do no such thing. You almost died from your injury and are not well enough for bedroom sport. I'm going now; do not try and stop me. I shall not share your bed until the stitches have been removed by the doctor and not by your overexertion.'

He waved airily towards the curtains. 'You must do as you wish; after all I am an accommodating husband. But I think it might be unwise to appear as you are. Penrose might never recover from the shock.'

She looked at her ruined garments and then tilted her head and pursed her lips. 'I would do so, my lord, if I had anything to put on.'

He reached behind him and produced his discarded nightshirt. He dropped it over her head and she hastily pushed her arms down the sleeves. It had barely reached to his knees but she was completely enveloped in the voluminous folds.

'Thank you, I am now respectable. However, I think it might be advisable for you to get Penrose to supply you with a fresh nightgown before the physician returns to see to that bleeding.'

Not waiting for him to respond she slipped between the curtains and ran pell-mell into her own domain. The thought that his valet would be well aware what had caused him to lose his nightshirt and open his wound made her hot all over with embarrassment.

Fortunately, Jenny was elsewhere and she found herself a fresh ensemble that did not require the attentions of a dresser to put on. Her abigail was happily reunited with her swain and would return with him when he left. Too much had happened these past few days and she needed time to adjust.

A long walk in the gardens would help soothe her troubled spirit and give her space to reflect. There was a pretty rose-covered arbour tucked away out of sight that would be ideal for contemplation. Once comfortably settled she reviewed the events of the past week.

Her husband had fallen in love with her, and then had nearly died saving the life of a village child. Her brother and cousin were going to Spain. Beau to search for Perry and Beth to marry her handsome lieutenant. She had decided to run away and then changed her mind.

She sighed and inhaled the delightful aroma of the roses. It had been an eventful week and she sincerely hoped that life would not be quite so exciting in the future. She smiled as she recalled that Harry had called himself 'an accommodating husband' – if that were true then she had sadly mistaken the matter. He was loving, intelligent, kind, but accommodating – that did not suit at all.

As she relaxed in the late afternoon sunshine she realised she owed her happiness to her cousin. If Beth had not attempted to elope none of it would have happened. She was the luckiest young lady in the country and also the happiest.

* * *

MORE FROM FENELLA J. MILLER

A Rebellious Bride, the next breathtaking Regency romance in The Duke's Alliance series from Fenella J. Miller, is available to order now here:

www.mybook.to/RebelliousBrideBackAd

ABOUT THE AUTHOR

Fenella J. Miller is the bestselling writer of over eighteen historical sagas. She also has a passion for Regency romantic adventures and has published over fifty to great acclaim. Her father was a Yorkshireman and her mother the daughter of a Rajah. She lives in a small village in Essex with her British Shorthair cat.

Sign up to Fenella J. Miller's mailing list for news, competitions and updates on future books.

Visit Fenella's website: www.fenellajmiller.co.uk

Follow Fenella on social media here:

facebook.com/fenella.miller
x.com/fenellawriter

ALSO BY FENELLA J. MILLER

Goodwill House Series

The War Girls of Goodwill House

New Recruits at Goodwill House

Duty Calls at Goodwill House

The Land Girls of Goodwill House

A Wartime Reunion at Goodwill House

Wedding Bells at Goodwill House

A Christmas Baby at Goodwill House

The Army Girls Series

Army Girls Reporting For Duty

Army Girls: Heartbreak and Hope

Army Girls: Behind the Guns

Army Girls: Operation Winter Wedding

The Pilot's Girl Series

The Pilot's Girl

A Wedding for the Pilot's Girl

A Dilemma for the Pilot's Girl

A Second Chance for the Pilot's Girl

The Nightingale Family Series

A Pocketful of Pennies

A Capful of Courage

A Basket Full of Babies

A Home Full of Hope

At Pemberley Series

Return to Pemberley

Trouble at Pemberley

Scandal at Pemberley

Danger at Pemberley

Harbour House Series

Wartime Arrivals at Harbour House

Stormy Waters at Harbour House

The Duke's Alliance Series

A Suitable Bride

A Dangerous Husband

An Unconventional Bride

An Accommodating Husband

Standalone Novels

The Land Girl's Secret

The Pilot's Story

You're cordially invited to

The Scandal Sheet

The home of swoon-worthy historical romance from the Regency to the Victorian era!

Warning: may contain spice 🌶

Sign up to the newsletter
https://bit.ly/thescandalsheet

Boldwood

Boldwood Books is an award-winning fiction publishing company seeking out the best stories from around the world.

Find out more at www.boldwoodbooks.com

Join our reader community for brilliant books, competitions and offers!

Follow us
@BoldwoodBooks
@TheBoldBookClub

Sign up to our weekly deals newsletter

https://bit.ly/BoldwoodBNewsletter

Printed in Dunstable, United Kingdom